TILL WE'RE TOGETHER AGAIN

When trouble struck her three daughters Ailsa MacFarlane found herself torn between them. Isobel, on holiday in Castildoro at her husband's archaeological dig, was caught up in a revolution, unable to return to their three children in Yorkshire. Dorrie, up in Scotland, was pregnant with twins following a previous miscarriage, while Kirsty had put her promising acting career and her relationship with Josh Elliott on hold, to care for Isobel's children. As Kirsty tried to comfort the three troubled children she was helped by their godfather Paul, a former boyfriend, but would she ever get her own life back on track again?

TILL WE'RE)GETHER AGAIN

Till We're Together Again

by

June Davies

Dales Large Print Books
Long Preston, North Yorkshire,
BD23 4ND, England.

British Library Cataloguing in Publication Data.

Davies, June
    Till we're together again.

    A catalogue record of this book is
    available from the British Library

    ISBN   978-1-84262-620-7 pbk

First published in Great Britain in 1996
by D. C. Thomson & Co. Ltd.

Copyright © June Davies 1996

Cover illustration by arrangement with
P.W.A. International Ltd.

The moral right of the author has been asserted

Published in Large Print 2008 by arrangement with
June Davies

Dales Large Print is an imprint of Library Magna Books Ltd.

Printed and bound in Great Britain by
T.J. (International) Ltd., Cornwall, PL28 8RW

Chapter One

So Far Apart

It still seemed so strange to be waking up without Douglas at her side. Sleepily pushing a hand through her hair, Isobel Blundell leaned across to switch off the alarm clock on the bedside table, her eyes resting on the photograph that stood there.

Douglas had included it with his first letter from South America. It showed him standing with the other members of the eight-strong team at the site of the sixteenth-century Spanish and Indian settlement they were excavating.

Isobel reached out to touch the picture with her fingertips, as if doing so might somehow bridge the miles and bring them closer.

Douglas was looking directly at her through the camera, smiling broadly, his blue eyes crinkling at the corners. Wearing shorts and sandals and a wide-brimmed hat, he looked tanned and fit...

'Mum?'

Alasdair came in quietly with Teddy bounding after him, her bottle-brush tail wagging furiously.

'What's the matter? Why are you up and dressed?' Isobel asked her son in a low voice. 'It isn't daylight yet!'

'There're badgers down by the beck. I saw their tracks in the mud yesterday!' he explained in an eager whisper. 'If I go while it's still dark, I might see them.'

'All right. But I'll make you a hot drink first.' She smiled, following him out on to the landing. 'Is Robbie up, too?'

'No. I don't want him to come, Mum,' Alasdair replied solemnly, starting soundlessly down the stairs in his thick socks. 'He's too little and he makes too much noise.'

'I doubt you'll need your binoculars today,' Isobel exclaimed a few minutes later, drawing the curtains back from the kitchen window.

Although snow still dusted the moors, the dark sky was low and brooding. A chill, heavy mizzle was rolling down from distant Hawksbeard Crag.

'Dad said it's best to always take them. Just in case,' Alasdair answered, drinking his chocolate as fast as the steaming liquid allowed. 'I wish he hadn't gone away, Mum.'

'We all do. And being away from us isn't nice for him, either,' Isobel straightened up from setting the fire and came to sit beside him. 'You haven't had another bad dream, have you?'

''Course not!' he declared, not altogether truthfully.

'If you do,' Isobel persisted gently, putting her arm about his shoulders, 'you're to come and wake me – understand?'

'I'm all right. I'm not a baby!' He wriggled away from her, stuffing his feet into his wellingtons. 'Dad would come back, wouldn't he? If we asked him to, I mean?'

'Yes. Yes, he would,' Isobel replied at once. 'But it means a lot that he was chosen to do this job in Castildoro. It's very important and it'd be pretty selfish of us to ask him to give it up and come home.'

'I still wish he was here, though.' Alasdair pulled on his new padded anorak.

'Me, too!' Isobel smiled as she wrapped a warm scarf around his neck. 'Now, away to your badgers. Be back in plenty of time for breakfast. And Alasdair–!' she called after him as the boy and dog dashed out into the cold, blue dawn light. 'Don't get muddy. You'll have to wear that jacket to school!'

Alasdair got back as she was dishing up breakfast, his new jacket soaked through and liberally spattered with slush.

'Do I have to wear this, Mum?' he grumbled later, tugging at the too-short sleeves of his old duffel coat as he wheeled his bike from the shed.

'It serves you right!' Isobel replied briskly, pulling the coat tight across the boy's narrow chest to fasten it. 'At least it's warm. I don't want you being ill again.'

She waved as Alasdair set off on the two-miles journey through the hilly lanes to Ferneys Beck village school.

As he disappeared from sight between the hedgerows she turned to her younger son.

'Come on, Robbie. It's freezing out here!'

Robbie came running, jumping and squelching, and they started up the steeply winding garden path. Above them stood the brown-stone house with its three tall chimneys, which gave it its name.

'Mum!' Robbie tugged at her hand. 'Can we make a cake today?'

'Good idea!' she agreed as she unlatched the door and shepherded him into the cosy kitchen.

Janey was still at the table, dawdling over

her toast and a fashion magazine. Isobel compressed her lips, glancing at the wall clock.

'Shouldn't you be on your way to school by now?'

'I've only a study period first thing.' Her daughter shrugged. 'It doesn't matter if I'm late.'

'Yes, it does,' Isobel answered shortly, beginning to clear the breakfast dishes. 'You'll find that out when you sit your exams next term! If you hurry, you'll still catch the bus into Cottingby.'

'But I told you, it's only a study–'

'Janey, I'm not going to argue with you!' Isobel interrupted sharply. 'Just go upstairs and get ready. And wash that make-up off your face!'

'Oh, Mum! You're so old fashioned!' Janey protested, her jaw jutting obstinately. 'Aunt Kirsty showed me how to put it on properly, and Amanda and all the other girls wear make-up to school!'

'It's fine at weekends,' Isobel replied, frowning at the palette of colours which had been her sister's most recent gift to Janey. 'But I don't want you wearing it to school!'

Janey scowled and complained, but she gave in relatively easily over the make-up.

Too easily?

Isobel considered her daughter's behaviour a while later when she and Robbie were baking. Would the cosmetics be hidden in Janey's bag so that the eye shadow and lipstick could be re-applied during the bus journey into Cottingby?

Well, you know your own tricks best! Isobel smiled sheepishly, remembering how she and her sister, Kirsty, had done just that when they'd gone dancing at the village hall in Auchlanrick, where Isobel's widowed mother, Ailsa, and youngest sister, Dorrie, still lived.

But their antics had just been high spirits whereas Janey – well, there had been times lately when Isobel had hardly recognised her daughter. Over the past couple of months, she'd changed from being such a happy, sunny-natured youngster...

'Robbie!'

Out of the corner of her eye Isobel saw him stretch up for the jar of golden syrup, but even as she darted towards him, the heavy glass jar tumbled from his hands and smashed on the hard floor.

'How many times have I told you not to do that? If you want something, ask for it! Now just look at this mess! Go into the sitting-room and stay there until I get the glass swept up!'

'But, Mummy, I don't want to–'

'Go! And find Teddy and keep her in there with you. We don't want her getting cut!'

The telephone rang while Isobel was still on her hands and knees mopping up syrup and glass with a damp cloth.

'Hi, Izzie!' The link with Castildoro was poor. Douglas sounded every inch of half a world away. 'I've been trying to call for two days, but you know what the phones are like here! Is everything OK?'

'Oh, I'm so glad to hear your voice! It's been–' Isobel began, then bit her tongue. It was hardly fair to bombard Douglas with domestic ups and downs the very instant he phoned. 'Yes, we're all fine!' she went on more cheerily. 'How's it going?'

'Better than we dared anticipate!' he responded loudly to be heard above the hiss and crackle. 'Yesterday, Angie – Angela Lennard, the young assistant I mentioned in my last letter? – unearthed a pot full of silver coins in near mint condition!'

'It must be very exciting!'

'Absolutely! I've been able to explore a little now, too,' he went on enthusiastically. 'It's beautiful country – and you'd adore the tropical flowers! I'm sending some pictures next time I write.'

Douglas paused, and for a moment neither of them spoke.

'I'm sorry I won't be there for your birthday,' Douglas said at last. 'At least Ailsa will be travelling down to spend a few days with you. And Kirsty's coming up from London, isn't she?'

'Yes. I'm looking forward to seeing them both – it's ages since we had a good natter,' she replied, although inwardly Isobel wasn't too sure that turning forty was a cause for celebration. 'I expect Kirsty will bring more presents for the children,' she went on. 'I'm sure she can't really afford it. And she spoils them dreadfully, racing about playing games, letting them do whatever they choose – then when she goes back to London, I'm left trying to settle three over-excited children back into a sensible routine!'

'Kirsty's always been full of energy, but I've never heard you grumbling about her before,' Douglas commented mildly. 'You sound as though you need to take a break.'

'How can I?' she demanded, her voice far sharper than she'd intended. 'I'm alone here with a family to care for and a home to run!'

'I wasn't ... say anything...' His sentences

were becoming disjointed as the connection began to break up.

'Douglas – I can't hear you!' Isobel cried in exasperation. 'Douglas–?'

The line howled and fell silent.

Regretfully Isobel replaced the receiver, filled with remorse at having snapped at him. But he'd sounded so excited and carefree and happy, while she... Sighing, she pushed a hand through her hair and returned to cleaning up the broken glass.

Wasn't he missing her – missing the children and his home at all?

Kirsty MacFarlane cycled through London's congested commuter traffic and turned off the busy main road. As she freewheeled into the narrow street of tall, Edwardian houses where she shared a third-floor flat, Josh Elliot jogged along the pavement beside her.

'You're cutting it fine!' He grinned. 'Aren't you going to Yorkshire this morning?'

She nodded and smiled. 'A place called Ferneys Beck. It's my sister's fortieth birthday.' She liked Josh, who had moved into the flat with her and Gwen, a singer, just a few weeks earlier. 'If I get to Euston on time!'

'Here, let me do that!' Effortlessly he carried the bike up the steps from the street.

'How many gears has this got?'

'Fifteen – but I haven't tried them all out yet!' Kirsty laughed, unlocking the door. 'I rode it in a French sportswear commercial and afterwards had the chance to buy it quite cheaply. It was too good a bargain to miss.'

Pushing the bike into the alcove under the stairs, they sprinted up to the flat and Kirsty dived into the bathroom to shower and wash her hair.

'Gwen, have you seen my ski-pants?' she called five minutes later, towelling her hair. 'The beigey ones that match my top with the roses on? I'm sure I left them around here somewhere.'

'Borrow my new leggings,' Gwen called, pausing from her breath control exercises. 'They'll match your top. Middle shelf in my wardrobe.'

'Great – thanks!' Kirsty returned with the leggings and cast an eye over the assortment of clothes strewn across her bed. 'I'm just wondering if I've got everything...'

'Enough for a world tour, I'd say!' Josh commented wryly, looking around the open door. 'May I come in?'

'Mmm, sure. Oh, could you pass me those two books from the shelf behind you?'

Josh handed her the paperbacks, glancing along the titles left still packing the shelf.

'Thackeray, Hugo, Brontë, Wilde ... I didn't even know you liked reading.'

'Love it!' She smiled, squeezing the books into a holdall.

'My boss has commissioned adaptations of about a dozen classic novels for the audio classics series we're releasing next year,' Josh commented.

'Oh?' Kirsty queried, a shade distractedly. She knew Josh was a sound engineer with one of the small independent recording companies, but that was about all.

'I've got Isobel's present, and Alasdair's. And Mum's lavender water. But there's still Janey's to go in...' She considered the floppy hippy-chick hat. 'It'll get crushed if I pack it – I'll just have to wear it. Then there are these!' She brandished a tiny pair of multi-coloured roller boots. 'Snazzy, eh? They're for Janey, too.' She laughed, spinning the red plastic wheels. 'I'd whizz along to the Tube in a flash on a set of these!'

'Talking of which, how are you getting to Euston?' Josh asked, lending his weight to the bulging suitcase that Kirsty was attempting to shut.

'I'll call a taxi.'

'You'll never make it. I'd be glad to take you.'

'We-ell, thanks...' Kirsty hesitated at the prospect of weaving, laden with luggage, across London in the rush-hour on the back of Josh's motorcycle.

'Do you want to catch your train or not?' he persisted with a grin. 'When I first came to London, I worked as a courier. There isn't a shortcut I don't know!'

Josh was as good as his word, and they reached Euston in plenty of time.

He went with Kirsty to her carriage, helping her stow her bags and sitting beside her. Now the rush was over, there didn't seem much to say.

'I'm doing a session with a choral group today,' he commented at length.

'That'll make a change from heavy metal,' she returned with a teasing smile.

'Quieter, anyhow!' he agreed, adding lightly, 'You won't forget to come back to us, will you?'

'With Violetta coming up? No way!' she retorted, then laughed when she saw his blank expression. 'Oh, of course, you don't know about it, do you? There's to be a tele-vision version of Alexandre Dumas's Lady of The Camellias, and my agent has managed to get me an audition.'

'Fantastic!' Josh exclaimed, genuinely delighted. 'You'd be great as Violetta.'

'You're too kind,' she replied warmly. 'This is the biggest opportunity I've ever had. I'll need to work hard to make the most of it.' She raised an eyebrow, indicating her holdall. 'I have copies of the script, the play, the novel in French, the novel in English, a video of the Hollywood silent movie. And my niece has volunteered to coach me – so I'll be nothing if not prepared! I want this role, Josh. I really want it,' she confided earnestly. 'I can't seem to think about anything else.'

Guards were slamming doors, a whistle blew, and Josh rose hurriedly.

'I'd better get off or I'll be coming with you!'

He paused, and quite suddenly Kirsty realised he was about to kiss her.

It wasn't just a polite kiss on the cheek, either. The warm tenderness of Josh's embrace took her unawares, lingering in her mind hours later when she was settling into her room at Chimneys.

'Cold milk and gingerbread still your favourites?' Isobel asked, appearing with a

19

laden tray. 'I thought we might have a snack and a natter. Mum has commandeered my kitchen!'

Kirsty looked up from unpacking her suitcase and smiled.

'Yes, please! Here's the only place I ever get home-baking.' She cleared a space on the bed to sit down. 'Isn't Mum looking well?' she commented. 'Pity Dorrie couldn't have come down with her, though.'

'Graham won't let her out of his sight.'

'Quite right, too!' Kirsty chuckled, continuing more seriously, 'I hope it all goes right for them this time. They're longing for a family – and Mum will be overjoyed to have another grandchild.'

'Especially one living under the same roof!' Isobel put in, smiling across at her. 'It's lovely having you here again, Kirsty. I'm awfully pleased you could come.'

'Is everything all right?' Kirsty ventured after a moment. 'You seem a bit fed up.'

'I'm fine. Well – I'm just being silly,' Isobel returned practically. 'It's just – I haven't heard from Douglas today. I know telephoning from Castildoro is difficult, but I haven't even had a card from him. When the postman brought an air mail envelope at lunchtime, I thought ... but it was from his parents in Canada.'

'In all these years, has Douglas once forgotten your birthday?' Kirsty demanded and went on to answer her own question. 'No, he hasn't – so he's not likely to start forgetting now, is he?'

'He's terribly busy and preoccupied...' Isobel replied uncertainly but Kirsty just scoffed.

'Rubbish!' She turned away to rummage through her bags. 'Anyway, this is for you from me. Happy birthday!'

'Oh, thanks. I'll keep it till tea-time!'

Kirsty cleared her throat.

'Er, you might prefer to open it now,' she suggested, her green eyes shining mischievously. 'While the children and Mum aren't around!'

Isobel's eyes widened. 'What on earth have you got me?'

'Open it and find out!'

Isobel carefully removed the pretty floral-patterned paper and opened up the box to reveal a frothy concoction of silk, lace and ribbons.

'A nightie set!' she gasped, smoothing her fingertips across the silky fabric and shaking out the folds to hold it up. 'You shouldn't have! It must've been ever so expensive. It's so extravagant ... and frivolous!'

'Isn't it, though?' Kirsty agreed blithely. 'I got it in Paris. Do you like it?'

'Like it?' Isobel echoed. 'It's the loveliest thing I've ever set eyes on!'

'Good! Now, why don't you take a long, leisurely bubble bath and get into the birthday mood?'

'I can't.' Isobel shook her head. 'Mum's busy in the kitchen, so I'll have to keep the children out of her hair and–'

'Leave them to me,' Kirsty chipped in briskly. 'I'll take them out for a few hours. It's a lovely day. We'll have lots of fun.' She was already on the landing and skipping lightly downstairs. 'Enjoy your bath and we'll see you at tea-time!'

'Close your eyes, Mummy. It's a surprise!' Robbie announced later that afternoon, taking Isobel's hand and leading her into the sitting-room overlooking the river.

Opening her eyes, Isobel exclaimed at the huge iced cake, glowing and flickering with dozens of tiny pink candles.

'Gran baked the cake,' Janey told her. 'But we made the icing ourselves.'

'And the letters,' Alasdair put in.

'I mixed the stuff for the letters!' Robbie

declared proudly.

'That's why they're navy blue!' Janey said with a long-suffering sigh. 'He put in a whole bottle of colouring.'

'Navy blue's my favourite colour, Robbie!' Isobel reassured him swiftly, ruffling the little boy's hair and gazing at the heap of packages and homemade envelopes arranged next to her plate.

'My goodness, are all these for me, too?'

'They're from us and Gran and Aunt Kirsty, but these are from Dad,' Janey explained. 'He didn't want to risk posting them, so he gave your card and present to me before he went away.'

'This is from Douglas, too.' Ailsa Mac-Farlane offered a bulky packet. 'He asked me to arrange it.'

Isobel's hand flew to her lips as she opened the packet and an airline wallet slid out on to the tablecloth.

'It's a ticket for me to go to Castildoro!'

Chapter Two

Castildoro

Castildoro was drowsing beneath the hot morning sun, nothing moving at a pace any quicker than that of the weary donkeys laboriously carrying their burdens of oranges, sugar cane, cotton and cocoa beans along the dusty streets.

'It may be the capital city, but everything happens *mañana* in Castildoro!' Douglas Blundell joked, his arm about Isobel's waist as they explored on the first full day of her holiday. 'But it's never less than enthralling. Just look around you – so much history! Portuguese, Spanish, Indian... Did you ever see such a mixture of cultures?'

'It's fascinating!' Isobel breathed, hardly able to absorb the unfamiliar sights and sounds.

Douglas led her up half a dozen marble steps into the shady arcades of a long-deserted colonial Spanish mansion. Its crumbling verandas spilled tangles of vivid, hugepetalled blooms that buzzed and hummed with insects.

'So how do you like Castildoro?' He smiled, drawing her closer.

Isobel leaned contentedly against Douglas's shoulder and exhaled slowly, drinking in the colours and contrasts.

'Even from your letters and photos, I never expected it to be quite so – foreign! And somehow, it feels almost as though time has stood still here.'

'Castildoro's filled with echoes from bygone ages,' Douglas agreed, his sun-tanned face breaking into a broad grin. 'Including our hotel! But seriously, it's a very poor country that's only just emerging from over seventy years of dictatorship. During the regime of General Ortega particularly, all resources were channelled into strengthening the army and increasing Ortega's personal power and wealth.'

Isobel took Douglas's hand as they strolled onwards through the dazzling sunshine.

'President Rosales is a good man,' Douglas continued, a frown touching his forehead. 'But there's an undercurrent of resistance to his plans for democracy.'

'Why?' Isobel murmured.

She'd been deeply moved by the memorial

which Douglas had shown her earlier. Just a simple, rough-hewn wall, bearing hundreds of names, its niches offering candles, ribbons and posy tributes to the men and women who had given their lives during Castildoro's long and bitter struggle for freedom.

'General Ortega still commands a lot of support,' Douglas told her frankly. 'Especially in the military and amongst those landowners who rely on peasant labour to operate their plantations.'

Isobel nodded, holding tightly on to his hand as they walked across Castildoro's town square with its small white church and water fountain. A tousle-haired boy was standing on tiptoe to drink from the tin cup chained to the stone-carved pump.

'He reminds me of Robbie!' Isobel whispered. 'I wonder what he and the others are doing right now?'

'Probably wondering what we're doing!' Douglas laughed. 'I wish we could have brought the children over – although I can hardly believe you're actually here! I was half afraid you wouldn't use the ticket.'

'Mum had let them in on the secret and they were thrilled to bits about surprising me with it.' Isobel swallowed the lump which came unexpectedly to her throat. 'They helped me pack and organise everything. And they've all promised to behave while Mum's looking after them. Even so, I did wonder about coming,' she admitted softly, reaching up to touch Douglas's cheek. 'But now we're together again… Oh, you'll never know how much I've missed you!'

It was early afternoon before they returned to Castildoro's hotel. A Jeep, driven by a pretty, auburn-haired young woman, drew to a halt beside them and a man of around forty, wearing dust-stained shorts and work shirt, climbed out.

'Hey, Karl!' Douglas greeted him. 'You haven't met my wife.'

Douglas turned and gave Isobel's waist a squeeze.

'Darling, this is Professor Karl Fischer from Clayman Groves University in New York. And Angela Lennard, his assistant,' he added as the smiling young woman came towards them. 'Angie – this is my wife, Isobel. We were about to find some iced tea. Won't you join us?'

'Yes. Yes, very well,' Karl Fischer agreed agitatedly, not even waiting until they were seated around a table in the hotel's lobby before turning to Douglas.

'The Soler brothers didn't show up at the

site this morning. And one of our station-wagons and some of our camping equipment have disappeared.'

'We depend heavily on local labour, Isobel,' Angela explained. 'Enrique Soler is our foreman, and his three brothers are amongst our most trusted workers. Or had been,' she amended.

'This is totally out of character for any of them. As for them being thieves–' Douglas shook his head. 'I can't believe that. We must talk to them, hear their side.'

'I drove out to their village. They aren't there,' Angela added. 'I'll have to report the theft to the police. I'll ask if they know where the Solers are.'

Douglas considered for a moment.

'You might learn more by asking Sam Fraser, Angie.'

Isobel noticed the glance which passed between them at the mention of the Scotsman whom she'd met at dinner the previous evening. She understood he was a pilot of some sort, and not in any way connected with the excavation.

After Angela hurried away, the earnest discussion continued between Douglas and Karl Fischer, and it became evident to Isobel that Douglas was needed back at the dig.

'I don't want to leave you already!' Douglas protested quietly.

Isobel shook her head.

'Don't worry about it. I may be on holiday, but I know you've still got to work. Besides, I'm not used to this heat yet. It'll suit me fine just to have a bite of lunch and then relax.'

Suitably reassured, Douglas went off with Karl Fischer leaving Isobel to her own devices.

The hotel proprietor had very little English and Isobel couldn't speak Spanish, so the two were muddling through good-naturedly as she tried to order lunch when a friendly voice spoke up behind her.

'May I help, Mrs Blundell?'

Sam Fraser had sauntered into the dining-room, hanging his sun-bleached panama on the hat-rack, and she greeted him with undisguised relief.

'Please!'

In a matter of minutes he had translated what it was she wanted into an order that the proprietor could understand, and then they both sat back and exchanged polite smiles.

'The food's better than you might expect,' Sam commented as they waited for their order. 'Cooking is Hector – the proprietor's – favourite pastime.'

'Have you been staying here long?' Isobel inquired.

'Castildoro – and this hotel – have been home for longer than I care to remember.'

Isobel returned his smile, and when Sam didn't say anything more, she mentioned the problems at the dig.

He nodded. 'Angela Lennard caught up with me at the airstrip. All I could tell her was that the site isn't the only place losing men, but I'll keep an ear to the ground.'

They continued to chat in a general kind of way about the dig and the country, and about Sam's work as a pilot.

'After leaving the RAF, I flew in Australia. On the mail-and-medicine run, as it was called back then,' he related wryly. 'Then I moved on to Oahu, ferrying tourists around the Hawaiian Islands. What a job that was!'

'What brought you to Castildoro?' Isobel asked, cautiously sipping a glass of the rough, sweet local wine that he had ordered for her.

'Oh, circumstances,' Sam grinned, dismissing her question. 'I'm still willing to fly anyone, or any cargo, that needs to fly. Although these days–' He stared into his glass, the humour ebbing from his face. '–I mostly while away my time swapping stories and playing cards with Hector.'

Her conversation with Sam Fraser was still in Isobel's thoughts later that evening, when she and Douglas were walking in the fragrant coolness of the moonlight.

'Mr Fraser hardly seems happy in Castildoro. And he doesn't have family or roots here. So why does he stay?'

'I've no idea,' Douglas replied rather shortly. 'He certainly seems to know everybody – and everything that goes on.'

'You don't like him, do you?'

'There's something about him that just doesn't add up.' His face relaxed into a smile. 'On the other hand, he's well liked and respected by everyone I know, while Angie says he reminds her of Clark Gable.' He pretended to scowl. 'I'm not sure I care for you having lunch with a man like that!'

'Are you jealous?' she replied coyly.

'Who – me?' he began, then laughed softly. 'Of course I'm jealous!'

He bent to kiss her as they passed beneath the shadowy archway into the square, then as he raised his head his eye fell on the man in question.

'Speak of the devil!' he muttered drily, indicating the cantina where he could see Sam Fraser sitting outside playing cards. 'I ought to go and have a word with him, all the same.'

Sam answered Douglas's inquiry without raising his eyes from the cards.

'You've seen the last of the Soler brothers, your station-wagon and your camping gear – they were spotted heading south towards Vargas.'

'That doesn't make any sense,' Douglas countered stiffly. 'Why would they leave their families and become thieves simply to travel two hundred and fifty miles to a place that's been a virtual ghost town since Ortega's defeat? There's nothing down there but swamp and ruins!'

'I wondered about that myself, so I flew over the place earlier this evening and took a look,' Sam returned. 'There must be nearly twenty men living under canvas on what's left of Ortega's old army training camp.'

There was silence as Douglas took this in.

'Even if that's so,' he replied at length, 'the camp is close to the border. Those men might be crossing as illegals and picking up lucrative work at the machine tool plant.'

'For all our sakes, I hope you're right.'

Sam's tone was lightly mocking. 'Personally, I doubt it. And it's also my personal opinion–' He glanced up for the first time, meeting Douglas's eyes steadily. '–that you were a fool bringing your wife to a place like Castildoro!'

Sitting in the north London rehearsal rooms, Kirsty kept her head bowed over the Lady of the Camellias script. At auditions, she found that watching the others reading for the part only added to her nerves.

'Kirsty!' A tall man with a greying beard edged along the row of wooden seats towards her. 'Long time no see!'

'Robert!' she exclaimed in a whisper. Robert Cox had been in the cast of Kirsty's very first play after leaving drama school. 'How are you?'

'Can't grumble,' he replied. 'Well, I could – but I won't!'

'Are you trying out for Alfredo?' she asked.

'I'm reading for the good doctor,' Robert answered with a wry grin. 'I'm far too old for dashing romantic heroes. Fathers, stolid businessmen and figures of authority are my line now.'

'You were terrific in that law series,' she

responded sincerely.

'That show'll run for ever,' Robert commented. 'I would've been in steady work until I retired if they hadn't insisted on killing me off. No such thing as job security, is there?'

'No, there isn't,' Kirsty agreed with considerable feeling.

She'd been fortunate not to be out of work for more than a few weeks during the past year, but she dreaded unemployment. Aside from the financial anxieties, it was incredibly frustrating. She just couldn't abide being idle and unable to work.

'Kirsty MacFarlane?' someone called. 'Kirsty MacFarlane!'

'Well, this is it!' Kirsty muttered, taking several deep breaths as she rose from her seat.

'Just like hearing your name called at the dentist, isn't it?' he returned with a wry smile.

Kirsty trailed despondently up the three flights of stairs. The instant she shut the front door, the flat's dull emptiness closed in around her. Gwen was away for the summer season and it was Josh's evening at the local talking newspaper.

She sighed heavily, kicking off her shoes and flopping down on to the orange and purple sofa. The room was horribly untidy; they'd been too busy this week to do much housework.

Not that it looked attractive even when it was tidy, Kirsty reflected bleakly. The flat was rented. The ghastly furniture, too. It was practically impossible to rent a halfway decent flat in London without its being furnished.

She got up again, too restless to be still. Perhaps a trip to the gym to work out the nervous energy would do the trick. She was pulling a clean tee-shirt and shorts from the drying line over the bath when the click of Josh's key sent her darting to the front door.

'Kirsty! What happened at...' His words trailed away as he saw her crestfallen expression. 'Oh, sweetheart, are you OK?'

'Not really,' she replied with a small smile. 'I could do with a hug!'

He opened his arms and Kirsty went to him, leaning her head against his chest.

'Do you want to talk about it?' he asked, stroking her hair.

'Not really,' she replied, then went on fiercely, 'It's all my own fault! I made the fatal mistake of letting myself imagine what it would be like to actually get the role.'

After another minute, she moved away a little, gazing up into his face.

'You're back early. Have you finished recording already?'

He shook his head. 'We'd hardly got started when one of the machines began playing up. I just slipped out while it's being repaired. I ought to be getting back, but I don't like just going off when you're so unhappy.'

'Nonsense!' she exclaimed with an immediate smile. 'Give me another hug and I'll be fine!'

After Josh left, the flat seemed drearier than ever. Kirsty stood gazing out to the grimy city street with its lines of traffic going nowhere and scurrying crowds trying to get somewhere, and in her mind's eye she could picture the space and freedom of the wild, windswept moors that rolled away beyond the windows of Chimneys...

Impulsively tapping out the number, she waited some while before the telephone was finally snatched up.

'Aunt Kirsty!' Janey gasped, dropping her satchel on to the hall floor. 'Phew – I thought the phone was going to stop before I got to it!'

'Isn't Gran there?'

'She's at the bottom of the garden picking gooseberries with Alasdair and Robbie,' Janey answered, then went on, 'How did it go? I told Amanda and the girls about your audition today. I bet you got the part, didn't you?'

'I don't think so.'

'Did you forget your lines or something?'

'No, it actually went fairly well,' Kirsty replied truthfully. 'I did my best – but sometimes your best just isn't good enough.'

'But we worked so hard!' Janey protested indignantly.

Kirsty hesitated uncomfortably. She never flinched from facing her own failures, but letting her family down was always horrible.

'Well, even though Violetta fell through,' she began apologetically, 'I've got that part in the soap coming up.'

'Oh, yes.' Janey was indifferent. She never bothered watching the programme. None of her friends did.

'Hang on, Aunt Kirsty – Gran's coming. I expect she wants to tell you about Auntie Dorrie.'

'What about Dorrie? Janey? Janey?' But Janey had gone.

Ailsa MacFarlane picked up the telephone, her gaze following Janey as the girl flounced upstairs, her pretty face sullen.

'Kirsty? It's me, pet. Don't go fretting about Dorrie. She and Graham were pleased as Punch when they called earlier. You'll never guess – she's expecting twins!'

'Twins? That's wonderful! But–' Her happiness was tempered with concern. '–is she all right?'

'Dr Weir's satisfied that she and the babies are doing well.' Ailsa sounded calm, though inwardly she wished she could be in two places at once. 'We've no cause to worry.'

'Well! That's really wonderful!' Kirsty said warmly. 'Wait till Izzie hears!'

'I'll be glad when she's home.' Ailsa sighed.

'There's nothing wrong, is there?' Kirsty asked. 'You're managing all right?'

'Of course!' Ailsa returned impatiently. 'The children are being as good as gold.'

'They're super kids.' Kirsty smiled. 'Izzie's a lucky woman.'

'Yes, she has many blessings,' Ailsa murmured, fancying she'd heard a brief wistfulness in her daughter's voice. 'Having a career is all well and good in its way,' she went on quietly, 'but isn't it time you started thinking of putting down roots of your own?'

Kirsty was quietly thoughtful for a few moments.

'I'll admit there are occasions when I think of Isobel … with Douglas and the children … a lovely home … a place where she truly belongs…' Kirsty confided, her gaze moving across the inhospitable, untidy flat.

'I worry about you being on your own and living so far away,' Ailsa said gently.

'Oh, Mum, despite everything I love my work!' Kirsty exclaimed fervently. 'I couldn't ever give acting up. I just *couldn't!*'

Douglas Blundell was never more content than when he was totally absorbed in his work. Isobel had long understood that and took a genuine interest in what he was doing, so she was keen to see the site of the archaeological dig which lay a long and bumpy drive beyond the outskirts of the city.

She joined Douglas and the others in the back-breaking task of carefully scraping and brushing the stony, baked earth from what had once been the interior of a trading post. Occasionally she assisted Angela Lennard with the meticulous tagging, cataloguing and packing of the tools, pottery, Spanish coins and Indian ornaments.

As well as artefacts, a wealth of historical and scientific data was being assembled. As Douglas observed, the dig was posing as many questions as it was resolving!

'There had been Indians living around that area for a thousand years before the Spanish arrived,' he was explaining late one night as he and Isobel were driving into Castildoro. 'And then – they left.'

'So why was it suddenly abandoned?' she asked with genuine interest. 'Was there a battle? Or an epidemic of some sort?'

'We're long on theories and short on evidence,' Douglas concluded, helping her down from the Jeep and catching hold of her fingers as they started into the hotel.

'I can scarcely believe that in less than a week all this will be a memory!' Isobel sighed, gazing up at him. 'I'll be back in Yorkshire, and we'll be apart again – until Christmas.'

He took her hand and tucked it under his arm, pulling her closer to his side.

'I hate being away from you and the children, you know that. I wish I could come home with you.'

'If you've any sense, that's exactly what you'll do!'

As Sam Fraser's curt voice spoke directly behind them, Isobel and Douglas spun around.

'We have to talk. Over there will do.' Sam

strode past them. 'We won't be overheard.'

Douglas and Isobel exchanged mystified glances, but followed Sam to the alcove with its well-worn couches.

'Why the drama?' Douglas inquired. 'What's going on?'

'Trouble.'

'Ortega?' Douglas's tone was abrupt. 'I don't suppose there's any point in asking the source of your information?'

'You don't need to know. Just accept that it's accurate,' Sam answered, turning to Isobel. 'Our old dictator is staging a come-back, Mrs Blundell. And he'll have the entire military backing him up.'

Isobel looked wordlessly at Douglas, un-disguised fear in her eyes. She'd seen and heard enough during her holiday to have gained a very frightening impression of General Ortega.

To her dismay her anxiety was mirrored in Douglas's eyes.

'The people who support President Rosales want to hold on to democracy, Isobel. They've fought in the past – they'll fight again.' His voice was urgent. 'You'll have to go home. Immediately.'

'I'm not leaving without you,' she answered unsteadily. 'Either we both go – or we both stay!'

'Izzie, please!' He broke off, knowing she wouldn't be swayed.

The work at the site was at a crucial stage. If he were alone, Douglas would have taken a calculated risk and stayed to continue the excavation. But with Isobel here...

'Take my advice – get your team and pull out of Castildoro as fast as you can. And keep your plans quiet,' Sam advised, getting to his feet. 'The fewer people who know you're trying to leave, the safer you'll be.'

Douglas considered his options. Transport was basic and unreliable. Arranging travel in the usual way took time – time they probably no longer had. He would have to swallow his pride and ask a favour from a man he not only disliked, but didn't wholly trust.

'Will you fly us out, Sam? Isobel and me – and any of the team who want to go?'

Sam shrugged. 'I'll take you across the northern border. After that, you're on your own. Meet me at the plane an hour before sunrise. Not at the airstrip, though. In the clearing behind the cane fields.'

As she sat aboard Sam Fraser's plane, waiting to take off, Isobel opened her handbag and looked at the photograph she'd brought with her of the children.

'It's going to be all right, darling,' Douglas whispered reassuringly.

Isobel tried to smile. It had seemed unreal, terrifying, to steal from the hotel and through Castildoro's deserted streets at the dead of night. The indigo sky above the distant mountains was illuminated with quick bursts of light and short explosions of fire. Fighting must already have started.

The professor and Angela Lennard were flying out with them. The other five members of the excavation team had elected to continue their work.

In the half-light of dawn, Douglas checked his wrist-watch.

'I think I'll go and find out what's holding us up...'

He spotted Sam Fraser standing some twenty yards away at the edge of the clearing, staring back along a narrow fire road between the cane fields.

'We ought to have left half an hour ago!' Douglas said. 'What's the delay?'

'A spot of engine trouble,' Sam returned curtly. 'We'll soon be on our way.'

'Engine trouble?' Douglas repeated in disbelief. 'Then why aren't you working on it?'

His question was answered by an unlit

vehicle approaching along the fire road. Sam waved it on and, without another word to Douglas, sprinted back across the hard ground towards the plane.

An elderly gentleman was helped out of the vehicle and aboard the plane by his companion, a young man in his early twenties.

'My name is Bernaldez,' the old man introduced himself. 'My sincere apologies for keeping you all waiting,' he murmured graciously, settling stiffly into his seat. 'I am afraid I can no longer hurry – an unfortunate combination of old age and frail health. Perhaps this is why my grandson, Luis, has chosen medicine for his profession!'

Señor Bernaldez smiled at his own small joke, but his grandson neither smiled nor spoke. He didn't even raise his dark eyes to look at his fellow passengers.

Isobel caught Douglas's gaze in silent question, but all he could do was shrug helplessly. He knew no more about this than she did.

When the plane was finally airborne, Sam Fraser advised everyone to get some sleep. However, Isobel found it impossible to rest. Although her body was weary, her nerves were on edge and her mind was racing. She tried closing her eyes, but they flew open again as she heard again those sharp reports that had accompanied them as they left Castildoro. Only now, the gunfire seemed closer…

In that same split second, there was a dull thump. Nothing more remarkable than that – but the plane lurched and pitched.

Everyone was awake now. The cramped cabin was filled with shouts. Isobel heard Sam's voice from the cockpit.

'We've got a problem! I'll have to find someplace to put down.'

Douglas's arms tightened about her and Isobel tried to speak. But no words came.

The small plane plummeted from the dawn sky, in a rapid spiral of black smoke…

Chapter Three

'We Were Shot Down!'

'Isobel! Isobel, darling…?' Douglas's voice gradually seeped into Isobel's consciousness.

She stirred, attempting to open her eyes,

but the lids were too heavy.

'Douglas…?' she mumbled, struggling to dispel the muzziness.

'I'm here. I'm fine. Everything's OK,' he murmured, and she could feel his hand on her forehead. 'We're down. Safe and sound. We're all all right. Just lie still.'

Isobel drew an unsteady breath, thankful it was all over and that they were alive and together. Her head was spinning and she squeezed her eyes tighter shut, moving closer into the reassuring security of his arms.

When the dizziness subsided, she looked up, blinking against the glaring sunlight shafting through the gaping doorway.

'Douglas!' she gasped, reaching out to touch his shoulder and face, staring horrified at the blood on his skin and clothes. 'You're hurt!'

'Cuts and bruises, that's all. It looks worse than it is.' He took her cold hands and chafed them within his own rough palms. 'Do you think you can get up now? We've got to get out of here.'

Isobel heard voices and saw movement in the cramped cabin as Douglas helped her up the steeply angled floor to the doorway. With his grandson's assistance, Señor

Bernaldez was already scrambling out, but Angela Lennard was still in the shadowed rear of the cabin. Propped up against one of the seats, the younger woman was obviously in considerable pain. Karl Fischer was kneeling at her side.

'Perhaps I can help...?' Isobel paused in the doorway.

'No need.' Sam Fraser emerged from the cockpit carrying a battered grey metal case with red crosses on each side. 'Karl and I can manage. You get outside – and keep warm. Don't be fooled by the bright sun. The temperatures are pretty low at this time of day.'

'Right then, young lady!' Sam continued, transferring his attention to Angela.

Outside the plane, Isobel discovered that Sam was right. Despite the dazzling sun streaking the sky with vivid orange and pink, it was still very cold. A damp, penetrating mist was wisping from the slow-moving waters of a broad river that snaked across the flat plain below. She could hear the distant trees were alive with the shrieks and whistles of birds.

And that was all. Silence enveloped them. Not a whisper of a breeze, not a sound from the deep, brown waters in the river. Not a single sign of human life – except the plane.

It lay behind them, a faint trace of acrid smoke hanging on the motionless air. Standing there together, gazing over the empty miles of plain, forest and hills, Douglas and Isobel were both struck with the same frightened thoughts.

Douglas glanced down to her ashen face and tried to smile.

'All those birds!' He put an arm around her. 'Alasdair would be down there with his binoculars…'

'Yes! We must tell him–' The words tailed off and, in spite of the effort she made, her lips trembled. 'Oh, Douglas! The children…'

'They'll be fine. They weren't expecting you back until the middle of next week anyway,' he reassured her, 'and by then we'll both be on a flight home.'

Isobel nodded, resting her head against the strength of him.

'I can just imagine their faces, can't you?'

Although she'd smiled, her eyes were bleak and Douglas pulled her closer.

'I'm scared, too, I can't deny it,' he murmured against her hair. 'But the worst is over. If Sam had time to warn us he was making an emergency landing, he'll have had time to send out a mayday call. Help is probably already on its way,' he concluded optimistically. 'All we have to do is stay put until they find us.'

'I suppose so,' she agreed. Struggling to get a grip on herself, she turned to the practical, something she could do to distract her from her scared thoughts. 'I'd better clean those cuts. The first-aid kit is in my maroon holdall. Do you think it's safe...?'

'I'll get it.' He hugged her again. 'And a couple of sweaters at the same time.'

Isobel held her breath as Douglas climbed back inside the wrecked plane. It lay at an angle on its side, the metal and glass crumpled and shattered like a child's broken toy.

She turned away abruptly, not wanting to think about what might have happened if Sam Fraser had been a less skilful pilot.

Cesar Bernaldez and Luis were sitting hunched on the coarse, bleached grass not more than three or four yards from where she stood. They looked as cold and lost as Isobel felt.

Luis hadn't uttered a single word during the entire flight from Castildoro, but now he was speaking in rapid Spanish. He was underlining the urgency of his argument with quick gesticulations, his lean face animated, his dark eyes earnest.

Señor Bernaldez was listening with great patience to his grandson's emotional out-pourings. Occasionally he inclined his head, or made a mild observation. Isobel realised he was simply allowing Luis to expend the fear and anger that was boiling up inside him.

Although frail, Cesar Bernaldez seemed to have survived the crash remarkably well. But an hour or so later, when Isobel had helped make Angela more comfortable, she was shocked to find him pallid and drowsy, his head slumped forward to his chest.

Luis was trying to rouse his grandfather.

'Don't!' Isobel shouted, stumbling over the scrubby ground in her haste to reach the boy as he raised a silver hip flask to Señor Bernaldez's colourless lips. 'Don't let him drink!'

'I don't know what to do. Help him!' Luis pleaded. 'This is my fault. Because of me this happens to Cesar! Please – help him!'

As a young wife, Isobel had taken a first-aid course being run by the WI, and in the years since had often had cause to be grate-ful for the training. But with Cesar Bern-aldez she was out of her depth so she was relieved when Sam took over.

'Luis would have given his grandfather that brandy,' she reflected later to Douglas, shaking her head. 'Yet giving anything by mouth – especially alcohol – could've been fatal.'

Under Sam's care, Señor Bernaldez's condition had improved and he was resting as comfortably as possible under the make-shift awning, which sheltered him from the heat of the afternoon sun.

As she poured water into Sam Fraser's tin tea can and set it over the fire to boil, she glanced across to where Luis sat holding the old man's hand. Sam was with them, sitting on the ground and talking in low, grave tones.

Isobel frowned in perplexity as her eyes rested on the young South American.

'His grandfather said he was a medical student,' she concluded, 'yet he doesn't even know basic first-aid!'

'Hmm?' Douglas murmured absently. He was only half listening to her observations for he was concentrating hard on the map spread out on the dusty ground before him.

How far north from Castildoro had they actually flown? And how long might it be before they were rescued? According to this map…

Douglas glanced up as Sam Fraser joined them at the fire.

'Any chance of a cuppa, Isobel?' He grinned, but his tanned face was drawn and there were deep lines around his eyes.

'I'm making some for us all,' she assured him, indicating the assortment of flask cups, beakers and tin mugs she'd found in the wreckage. 'And there's the last of the sandwiches Hector packed for us.'

Sam nodded, rubbing his eyes with thumb and forefinger. It was the first sign of weariness he'd shown, and Isobel felt suddenly ashamed. While she and the others had been resting, Sam hadn't once allowed himself a break. The strain of the crash-landing, and the responsibility he obviously felt towards his passengers, had to be exacting a tremendous toll.

'Here you are,' she said quietly, placing a tin mug in his hands.

'Thanks. We've adequate dry provisions on board to tide us over,' he commented thoughtfully, glancing past her to the aircraft, 'and fresh water won't be a problem. Not in this area, at least.'

'How is Señor Bernaldez?' Isobel inquired after another moment.

'Not good,' he told her candidly. 'But old

and sick as he is, he's probably got more strength and courage than the rest of us put together. He says he'll be ready to move on in the morning – and he will.'

'Move on?' Douglas echoed sceptically, getting to his feet. 'Where to? And why? Surely it makes more sense to stay with the plane? A search party will sight the wreckage far more easily than it'll spot us.'

'And just who do you imagine will be looking for us?' Sam demanded, fatigue quickening his temper. 'This isn't Europe, Doug. There's no RAF or emergency services waiting to come rushing to our rescue out here!'

'I realise that.' Douglas stared levelly at him, his instinctive distrust of the man resurfacing. 'But you did have time to radio a distress message before the accident – didn't you?'

'For pity's sake, use your head!' Sam exploded angrily, tossing the dregs of his tea into the fire. 'It wasn't an accident that brought us down. Or engine failure or pilot error, either! We were shot down! Whatever's happening in this wretched country, we're caught right in the middle of it,' he concluded bitterly. 'And if we're to survive, we have only ourselves – and each other – to depend on!'

Kirsty exchanged a cheery good-morning with the milkman as she jogged past his rattling float, then, pausing for a breather on the seat beside the church, she inhaled appreciatively. She'd almost forgotten how cool and clean the air at Auchlanrick was.

The one-act play she was appearing in in Edinburgh had closed just the previous evening, and on the spur of the moment she had driven up to see Dorrie and Graham. Kirsty hadn't been back for a visit since the couple's wedding four – no, nearly five years ago.

Before she cooled down too much, she continued on round the churchyard, past the manse, and down the hill again to the old grey house where she and her sisters had been born and raised. It had scarcely changed in all those years and Kirsty felt glad, yet again, that after their marriage Dorrie and Graham had decided to live there.

Ailsa MacFarlane might be a sprightly woman with lots of friends, and she always kept busy, but she wasn't getting any younger, and Kirsty was glad she wasn't living alone.

Graham's painter and decorator's van was parked in the driveway alongside Kirsty's own ageing hatchback and he was loading his ladders on to the roof rack as Kirsty turned in at the gate.

'I noticed your handbrake cable was hanging loose under the car,' he commented as she paused to greet him. 'I've fastened it back up.'

'That was kind of you. Thanks, Graham.' Kirsty got down on her hands and knees and peered under the car. 'Yes, I see where you've fixed it. I hadn't noticed it.'

'Oh, it wasn't dangerous,' Graham assured her. He was a solid, hard-working young man, slow to speak out and never one to make a great fuss. 'But it was as well to tuck it out of harm's way, 'specially if you're to be driving over rough roads.'

'I'll certainly be doing that!' She laughed, straightening up and making for the house. 'I'm taking that short-cut through Scarswale Pass to Ferneys Beck tomorrow. I want to say hello to Mum and the kids before I head back to London.'

The front rooms of the tall house were dull in the mornings, but as Kirsty sprinted upstairs sunlight was flooding on to the narrow landing from the wee back bedroom. It had been Dorrie's when she was a little girl, but Graham had redecorated it as a nursery.

'Dorrie! You shouldn't be doing that!'

Kirsty had glanced through the open doorway to see her younger sister standing on tiptoe on a low footstool, stretching up to hang a gaily-coloured mobile above the cradle.

'You sound just like Graham,' Dorrie protested mildly. 'He fusses, too.'

'I'm not surprised! You shouldn't be climbing about the furniture in your condition. Here – let me.'

Kirsty took the mobile and carefully finished hanging it. Then they both stepped back to admire it.

'There – oh, it's super, Dorrie!'

'It came this morning. I sent away for it. I know it's far too soon to put it up, but I just wanted to see what it looks like. There was a Jack-in-the-box design, too, but I kind of liked the rabbits.'

Dorrie sat back heavily on the padded lid of the cream ottoman and gazed content-edly around the room. Then, suddenly, her smile vanished.

'You don't think I'm tempting fate, do you? Graham and I had this room all ready last time. And I'd knitted–' She broke off, catching her lower lip between her teeth. She'd never confided in anyone, not even Graham, about the many times she'd crept in here and hugged that little matinee jacket to her, weeping alone for their lost baby.

Graham had been a tower of strength, but it wasn't his way to show his grief. He'd never mentioned the miscarriage after it was over.

'You've heard the old saying about preparing a nursery–'

'You don't believe that nonsense, do you?' Kirsty interrupted.

'No. No, of course I don't. Not really,' Dorrie answered, her smile returning.

She leaned forward to smooth her fingertips along the side of the wicker cradle, rocking it gently.

'It's just that, sometimes, when I'm ironing or washing-up or something, I'll catch myself imagining what it'll be like after the babies are born.' She folded her hands across her middle. 'Graham and me bathing the twins ... putting them to bed ... doing all the ordinary, everyday things... We've dreamed of having a family for such a long time. I just can't believe it's really going to come true.'

Kirsty gulped, swallowing the knot of emotion in her throat as she met her sister's eyes. Dorrie looked so young – young and bonnie and glowing with the promise of new life.

'But it is going to come true,' Kirsty insisted, reaching across to pat Dorrie's hands. 'And in just a couple of months, too!'

'Seven weeks and five days,' Dorrie corrected, her eyes shining. 'I tick each day off. They could've told us if the twins are boys or girls – or one of each – but I didn't want to find out that way. I think it's nicer to wait until you see your babies, don't you?'

'I'm not sure, I've never thought about it.' Kirsty laughed. 'Pregnancy suits you, Dorrie. I've never seen you looking happier.'

'I thought I'd never be happy again. But I am,' Dorrie replied simply. 'Oh, I get nervous, too. Graham's taken on a lot of extra jobs so he can have time off after the twins are born, so he's out from early till late every day, even weekends, and what with Mum being down at Izzie's... Well, sometimes when I'm on my own, I feel scared. It's silly, because if there was a problem while Graham's out–' she reasoned sensibly, '–I've good neighbours who'd help. But...'

'But it's not like having Mum here with

you, is it?' Kirsty put in understandingly.

Dorrie ruefully shook her head. There was a big age gap between her and her two sisters so that Isobel and Kirsty had already been grown-up and living away from home when their father had died, but Dorrie had still been a little girl, so that she and Ailsa were especially close.

'I'll be so much happier when Mum gets back next week,' she admitted. 'But don't tell her I said that, will you? I don't want her worrying.'

Kirsty laughed. 'No chance of that! Mum'll still be worrying about us when we're collecting our pensions!' She inclined her head to consider her sister. 'Have you had breakfast?'

'No. I cooked for Graham, but it was so early I didn't feel like anything myself.'

'Have you any strange cravings for burnt toast and rubbery porridge?'

'No, I haven't!' Dorrie exclaimed indignantly.

'That's too bad.' Kirsty extended her hand to help her sister rise from the low ottoman. 'Because they're about the only things I can cook!'

'I've never had pancakes for breakfast

before,' Dorrie commented later, and narrowed her eyes consideringly across the table at Kirsty. 'You know, I think you could be a really good cook if you put your mind to it.'

'I don't really have the chance. The flat's kitchenette doesn't have a proper cooker. At least, that's my story and I'm sticking to it!' Kirsty grinned. 'Josh showed me how to make the pancakes.'

'What's he like?' Dorrie asked conspiratorially, cupping her hand under her chin and leaning on the check-clothed table. 'You're really keen on him, aren't you?'

'Terrific. And maybe!'

'Maybe my eye!' Dorrie snorted disbelievingly. 'You get a funny look in your eyes whenever you mention his name. Have the two of you got any plans?'

'Plans? You're as bad as Mum!' Kirsty protested amiably. 'Josh *is* special, and we'd love to spend more time together, but work keeps us apart. While he's in London, I'll be away doing a play or something, and if I'm in town for a spell, as often as not he'll be off recording, or producing in Europe. Mostly we just snatch – moments.'

'It must be awfully lonely. I couldn't live that way,' Dorrie said with a firm shake of her head. 'But at least you and Josh aren't married. I often wonder what Izzie was thinking about, encouraging Douglas to go off to South America like that. I mean, when she comes back from her holiday, she won't see him again for more than six months! If my husband wanted to take a job halfway across the world, I certainly wouldn't back him up the way she did.'

'Yes, you would,' Kirsty returned knowingly. 'If the job meant as much to Graham as working at Castildoro does to Douglas, you would.'

Looking unconvinced, Dorrie got up to fetch a newspaper from the magazine rack.

'Have you read the article about Douglas in *The Cottingby Herald?* Mum sent it to me,' she said, leafing through the paper and folding it open at the right page. 'There're pictures of some of the things they've found.'

Kirsty shook her head. 'Isobel told me what Douglas was doing, but I haven't seen any pictures.'

She began to read with interest.

'Goodness, no wonder Douglas is so keen! Castildoro sounds incredible, doesn't it? Imagine finding an almost intact room with wine and letters and even a jar of pomade that belonged to whoever lived there centuries ago! It's incredible, isn't it?'

While Kirsty continued to pore over the paper Dorrie topped up their tea-cups.

'Mum sometimes mentions Paul when she phones,' she commented, when Kirsty had finished reading. Paul Ashworth had been Douglas's best man, and was godfather to the three Blundell children. 'Apparently he's been visiting two or three times a week, taking the boys to cricket matches, ferrying Janey to the ice rink and going to church with them – that sort of thing. Mum didn't really know him before, but she's got really fond of him.'

'He's a nice man.' Kirsty remarked evenly. 'And he's devoted to the children. Always has been.'

'Do you ever see him these days?' Dorrie ventured.

Kirsty shook her head. 'I'd heard about him coming home to take over the *Herald* after his father retired, of course, but when I'm staying with Isobel I suspect he stays away. And when I'm in the village, or Cottingby, I avoid places where I might bump into him.'

'Surely after all this while...?' Dorrie exclaimed. 'Couldn't you at least be friends? You were inseparable at one time.'

'It'd be impossible,' Kirsty admitted at length. 'Paul and I hurt each other far too badly for that.'

'I was a bit worried about how these would wash,' Ailsa MacFarlane remarked to Winifred Bell as she carried the bundle of loose covers in from the garden. 'But they've come up nicely!'

'Ay, they look grand!' Winifred glanced around from polishing the dresser. 'I'll give you a hand putting them on once I've dusted.'

She'd been coming up from the village twice each week to help in the house ever since Isobel and Douglas had moved into Chimneys as newlyweds, and over the years she had grown to care for the Blundells and their children as the family she and her husband, Harry, had always longed for but never had. Now she and Ailsa were getting the house ready for Isobel coming home.

'Remind me to fetch those jam jars for you later, Mrs Mac,' Winifred remarked, when she and Ailsa were zipping the chintz covers on to the sitting-room suite. 'They're in a tea-chest in the cellar.'

'Thanks. I used the last pot of strawberry in tarts for the children's lunchboxes,' replied Ailsa, pulling the frilled skirts into shape. 'And the garden strawberries aren't ready for picking yet, so Kirsty's taking the children – well, the boys; Janey doesn't want to go – to the soft fruit farm along the Beck.'

'Robbie'll enjoy that.' Winifred chuckled, getting stiffly up from her knees. 'But he always eats as many as he picks. The farmer'll have to weigh him as well as the baskets!'

'I'll come to the village with you, Mrs Bell,' Ailsa said later, when Winifred was fetching her cardigan and bag from the cupboard under the stairs. 'I want to do a bit of shopping before I collect Robbie from playschool.'

'Company'll make the walk seem shorter.' Winifred jabbed a stray pin back into her wiry, iron-grey hair. 'Because I swear, these lanes keep getting longer!'

'Have you always lived in Ferneys Beck?' Ailsa asked as they strolled beneath the shady willows along the river-bank.

'Except for a spell near Scarborough when the railway transferred Harry, but that was only temporary.'

'How is your husband?' Ailsa inquired. Illness had forced Harry Bell into early retirement.

'No better, poor man. He gets very down

in spirit,' Winifred answered bleakly, starting up the slope of the narrow, dry-stone bridge crossing the beck. 'He was always so strong and active but now there are some days when he can't even leave the house. It's hard for him to accept.'

They were just turning the corner by the village shop when Paul Ashworth's maroon car drew up a short distance ahead. He got out and walked back along the lane to meet them.

'Ailsa – Winifred – I was just on my way up to the house,' he began, then hesitated, obviously uneasy, and Ailsa looked at him curiously, waiting for him to go on.

As he glanced from her to Winifred, she began to feel concerned.

'What is it, Paul?'

Paul took a deep breath. 'Look – can we go somewhere? I need to talk to you – and I can't do it in the street.'

'What's happened, Paul?' Ailsa's voice was sharp with alarm. 'Is it one of the children?'

'No – no! Nothing like that.' Paul tried to soothe her. 'A chap from Castildoro – a mutual friend of mine and Douglas's – called me at the office,' he went on carefully, doing his best not to scare the women. After all, there might be no real cause. 'There's been some sort of rebellion and he left in a hurry. Douglas and Isobel tried to get out, too, but their plane never reached its destination...'

Chapter Four

'They're Not Coming Back!'

The night was hot and sticky; the rain had done nothing to refresh the oppressive air.

Ailsa lay awake, listening to the hall clock striking each passing hour. Finally she got up, put on her dressing-gown and went downstairs.

Switching on the light, she pushed the kitchen windows open and went into the pantry. The rows of clean jam-jars were still standing on the marble shelf, and next to them the strawberries Kirsty and the boys had picked.

All thoughts of jam-making had been pushed from Ailsa's mind by Paul's news, however.

'Missing' was how he'd described it, she remembered, carrying the berries through to the kitchen and mechanically beginning to sort them.

It seemed impossible to her that with all the sophisticated equipment available nowadays, even a small plane could just take off and disappear. But, as Paul had said, it was a very large country.

He had also said, trying to be reassuring, that there was bound to be a perfectly simple reason and that the plane would more than likely turn up safe at any one of a score of remote airstrips.

Suddenly the terror she'd been fighting to keep in check rose up, threatening to overwhelm her, and she gripped the edge of the table until her knuckles whitened.

'Mum?' Kirsty asked in concern, padding barefoot into the kitchen. 'You're surely not making jam now?'

Ailsa started, pulling herself together.

'The strawberries will be past it by morning. Besides, I'm better up and doing.'

'I'll help you.' Kirsty went over to wash her hands at the sink. 'Do you suppose Paul has got in touch with Douglas's parents in Canada?'

Ailsa looked stricken. 'I'd forgotten about them! I'd better phone!'

'I'll see to it,' Kirsty assured her gently,

noting her mother's jerky movements which conveyed an agitation Ailsa rarely displayed. 'You look all in. Sit down and I'll warm some milk.'

Meekly Ailsa obeyed.

'I know Paul said we shouldn't panic, but I just can't help it. They're lost, miles away from home in some foreign country I've hardly even heard of!' she cried, no longer able to contain her anguish. 'What if something terrible has happened to that plane? And Izzie and Douglas haven't managed to escape–'

She turned sharply, a movement catching her eye.

Alasdair had come quietly into the kitchen and was standing rooted to the spot, staring mutely at them.

Ailsa caught her breath, her mind racing. How long had he been standing there? How much had he overheard?

'Hello, love!' She forced a smile, trying to sound calm. 'What are you doing up?'

Alasdair's eyes were wide. He'd heard what she had said and although he opened his mouth and tried to say something, nothing would come out. All he could do was stand there. His legs wouldn't move either.

Seeing his shock, Ailsa rose and started

towards him, but at that the numbness suddenly released him and he shrank away, tears brimming.

'Mum and Dad aren't coming back!' he shouted, backing away from her. 'They're dead, aren't they? Aren't they?'

He didn't wait for an answer. Turning on his heel, he ran into the dark hall, wrenched open the back door so hard that it crashed back against the wall, and fled into the night.

'Alasdair!' Ailsa cried desperately.

'It's all right, Mum.' Kirsty was already crossing the kitchen and running through to the hall. 'I'll go after him.'

She raced out into the wet garden, and stopped, peering into the darkness. Pitch-black grass, bushes, trees ... Alasdair was nowhere to be seen.

Then she glimpsed the flash of the boy's light-coloured pyjamas moving swiftly beyond the hawthorns, and took off after him.

She caught up with him near the beck and grabbed his shoulders, pulling him around to face her.

'Alasdair!'

'Why didn't you tell us?' he cried bitterly.

'Listen to me! Your mum and dad are alive and they're coming back!' she insisted, holding on fiercely to his shaking shoulders. 'Their plane didn't show up where it should have,' she went on breathlessly, falling to her knees in the rain-sodden grass so that their faces were on a level. 'So we aren't sure where they've gone yet – but that's all!'

Alasdair's chest was heaving with exertion and rasping sobs. Tears mingled with the rain trickling from his fair hair and coursing down his cheeks. He said nothing, staring at her almost distrustfully. His body felt rigid beneath her grasp and she had to suppress an impulse to wrap her arms about him to comfort him. She sensed that any such gesture would send him shying even further away.

Slowly she dropped her hands from his shoulders, half expecting him to dart away again – but he stood his ground, making no move to run. His hurt blue eyes were locked unflinchingly on hers.

'Are you telling me the truth?' he demanded accusingly. 'Is that really what's happened?'

'Yes. I promise you, Alasdair. Their plane is missing,' Kirsty told him simply, wiping the sleeve of her pyjamas across her dripping face. 'Flights often get delayed, or diverted to other places, because of bad weather or –

oh, all sorts of reasons. I think that's what's happened to their plane. They'll be all right, Alasdair. You'll see.'

'Do you really think so? You're not just saying it because you think I'm not old enough to understand?' he persisted, his voice trembling. 'Mum and Dad always tell us things properly. Even really bad things, like when Mum had to have that operation.'

'If I knew anything, I'd tell you,' she said earnestly. 'As soon as Paul has some news, I will tell you. Everything.'

'Promise?'

'Promise.'

Alasdair studied her earnestly, suddenly looking very like Douglas. He scanned her face for a moment or two longer, before making up his mind and nodding decisively.

'All right. What do we do now?'

'Paul's trying to find out more, but things in Castildoro are so tricky, he said it could be a while.'

'Tomorrow?'

'Maybe the day after,' she admitted honestly.

'Paul'll find out where Mum and Dad are,' Alasdair said, with absolute trust and confidence in his godfather. 'They might even phone us from wherever they are, mightn't they? If they can get through, that is.'

He hovered uncertainly, shifting from one foot to the other, before taking that pace nearer. Kirsty reached out to touch his arm.

'Shall we go back inside now?' she asked quietly.

Alasdair nodded and fell into step beside her as they started slowly back towards the kitchen. Ailsa was at the window, watching anxiously for them.

'I don't want to go back to bed, Aunt Kirsty,' he murmured, looking up at her. 'I won't sleep.'

'I don't think I will either,' she agreed, slipping an arm about his shoulders. 'Suppose we fetch a couple of pillows and quilts and stay in the sitting-room tonight?'

After they had dried off, Kirsty made up a bed for Alasdair on the sitting-room couch, while she and Ailsa settled into the fireside armchairs. It was after three o'clock and Alasdair was curled up, his eyes almost closing, when the shrill of the telephone shattered the silence.

Ailsa was nearest and she snatched it up, but the voice she heard wasn't Paul Ashworth's, as she had expected, but Graham's.

'Ailsa, I'm at the hospital.' Her son-in-law was terse and anxious. 'It's Dorrie. She's ...

I think the babies are coming!

'Dorrie was feeling tired, so she went to bed early,' Graham explained distractedly from the hospital. 'Then the pains started.'

'So the babies are definitely on the way?' Ailsa's question was brusque with anxiety.

'We're not sure yet. The doctors are trying to put things right,' he replied tautly. 'They won't let me see her. But they've said the next few hours are critical. In the ambulance, she was fretting about you being so far away. You couldn't...?' He let the question hang in the air.

Ailsa thought quickly. Whatever was happening in South America, she couldn't help Isobel. But she could help Dorrie!

'I'll come as soon as I can. Kirsty's here at Chimneys, so she can stay with the children.'

As she hung up, Ailsa's shoulders sagged. Three-hundred-odd miles and several hours of travel separated her from her daughter. If only Auchlanrick wasn't so far away.

Alasdair heard her go slowly up the stairs and padded along the hall in his slippers to find Kirsty who had gone to his father's study.

'Aunt Kirsty? Gran looked so worried I

didn't like to ask,' he began, 'but what's wrong with Aunt Dorrie?'

'You know she's going to have a baby?' Kirsty replied, hastily rummaging through the desk for a train timetable. 'Babies,' she corrected. 'They're not due for nearly two months, but Dorrie's been taken to hospital. Graham and Gran are worried in case the twins are born too soon.'

'What'll happen if they are?' Alasdair asked, his eyes heavy from sleeplessness.

'They'll be very tiny,' Kirsty answered glancing up to see the worry on his face. She crossed the room to put her arm about his shoulders. 'They'll need lots of special care.'

'So Gran's going?' he murmured, his eyes large and forlorn. 'All the way to Scotland?'

'Mm-hm. But she'll only be gone a day or two,' Kirsty replied reassuringly, frowning as she opened the timetable. 'I can never make head or tail of these things. Can you?'

'Oh, yes.' He nodded confidently. 'Dad showed me ages ago. I'll look Gran's trains up for you.'

'Thanks.' She perched on the corner of the desk while Alasdair sat dwarfed in Douglas's large winged chair.

'You write down what I tell you.' Alasdair slid a pad and pencil across to her as he ran a finger down the index. 'Gran'll have to change about four times...'

'Oh, here you both are!' Ailsa said, coming into the kitchen a short while later. 'I'm ready.'

'Alasdair's looked up your trains.' Kirsty smiled, slipping the piece of paper into her mother's handbag. 'And he has a surprise for you.'

Alasdair handed Ailsa a bright blue plastic box.

'Mum always gives us a packed lunch when we go on a long journey. And I made a flask of tea, too.'

'This is very thoughtful!' Ailsa stooped to kiss him. 'Thanks, love. I'll be able to have breakfast on the train.'

Kirsty looked at her mother in concern.

'You've been up all night, Mum. Are you sure you'll be OK? Going all the way alone?'

'Oh, I'll be fine. I just want to get there and see Dorrie!' Ailsa replied, watching Alasdair going ahead of them into the hall and out of earshot. 'Kirsty,' she went on urgently, 'we haven't heard a word about Isobel and Douglas. Somebody must know *something*, surely?'

'I'm sure Paul's right – it's just poor com-munications,' Kirsty responded positively, helping her on with her coat. 'I've been trying to call Izzie's hotel since last evening, and I still haven't got through. The lines from Castildoro must be even worse than usual. The first train from Cottingby isn't till twenty past,' she went on, reaching for her own jacket.

Ailsa glanced up from checking her purse and frowned.

'What are you doing?'

'Going to get the car out,' Kirsty answered, taken aback. 'To run you to the station.'

'What about the children?' Ailsa reminded her, far more abruptly than she realised. 'You can't leave them alone!'

'No? No, of course not.' Kirsty shrugged ruefully. 'I hadn't thought about that.'

'We'll be all right, Gran.' Alasdair joined them at the door. 'I can look after Janey and Robbie while Aunt Kirsty takes you.'

'I'm sure you can.' Ailsa touched his hair. 'But I've already called Mr Deakin's taxi from the village.'

Dorrie was in hospital some eighteen miles beyond Auchlanrick itself. Ailsa started up the steps with a mixture of relief and apprehension. What had happened since she'd spoken to Graham all those hours ago?

He was sitting in the waiting area, his hands hanging loosely between his knees, elbows resting on his knees, but he jumped up when the lift doors opened and crossed the corridor towards her in a couple of strides. Tall and lanky, he looked very much younger than his twenty-four years.

'Ailsa! I'm so glad to see you! Dorrie's resting. I've seen her, though I don't think she knew I was there.' Graham rubbed his palm across his unshaven cheek. 'Mr Mapstone reckons she's out of danger – for the time being, at least.'

'Thank heavens!' Ailsa sank on to one of the plastic seats, suddenly weak at the knees. 'Graham – what about the babies?' she asked, her eyes on his face.

'We don't know. Not yet.' He looked away. 'There are all kinds of complications. She's very ill. The doctors were with her the whole night. I thought I was losing her–'

He broke off as the door of Dorrie's room opened. A nurse came out and approached them.

'Mr Mapstone will be along to check on Dorrie before he goes off duty.' Hannah Mackenzie smiled. 'She's sleeping, but I can give you a few minutes if you'd like to pop in. Just one of you, I'm afraid!' she added apologetically, as they both rose.

Ailsa immediately stood aside but Graham shook his head.

'I'm glad you're back,' he said simply, gesturing that she should go in.

Ailsa started to say she wasn't home for good, but seeing the fatigue and worry in his eyes, said nothing. Wrapped up in his distress for Dorrie, he couldn't be expected to think straight. He hadn't even asked after Isobel and Douglas yet, much less realised that Ailsa must go back to her grandchildren in Ferneys Beck. She merely nodded, stepping inside the single-bedded room.

Dorrie's thin face was ashen, her lips bloodless. She looked tiny and frail, connected up to a battery of tubes, machines and monitors. She wasn't awake but, as Ailsa stood beside the narrow bed, she stirred slightly and her eyes drowsily flickered open.

'Mum?'

'I'm here!' Ailsa whispered, leaning over to stroke her hair.

Comforted, Dorrie drifted back into sleep, while Ailsa continued to stroke her head, just as she'd done to comfort her when she was sickly or upset as a child.

Her heart ached at the thought of returning to Yorkshire and leaving Dorrie ill and afraid for her babies – but she had promised Isobel she'd look after her children...

Hannah Mackenzie popped her head around the door.

'I'm sorry, time's up! Mr Mapstone'll be along any second.'

Ailsa returned the nurse's smile and bent to kiss Dorrie's forehead before she rejoined Graham outside.

'She doesn't look too bad,' she murmured, more optimistically than she felt. 'She's sleeping comfortably.'

'That's a good sign. She needs to get some strength back. They've to do more tests later.' Graham sighed heavily, staring unseeing at the people passing along the corridor.

Presently, Mr Mapstone swept from the lift and past the row of seats where they were waiting, not appearing to notice them as he exchanged comments with the juniors at his side. The doctors turned into Dorrie's room, and as five, then ten minutes ticked by, Ailsa saw Graham looking up to the wall clock again and again.

'Mr Mapstone's only supposed to be checking on her!' he muttered at last. 'What's taking all this time? Why doesn't he come and tell us what's happening?'

Before Ailsa could reply, Nurse Mackenzie emerged from Dorrie's room.

'Would you come in, Graham?' she asked, and although her plump face was calm, almost without expression, there was no mistaking the urgency of her tone.

'But Dorrie's sleeping, isn't she?' he demanded, getting to his feet. 'What's gone wrong? Is it–?'

The nurse put a hand on his arm, firmly steering him inside. Before she followed, Hannah turned, her gaze catching and holding Ailsa's.

'The heartbeat of the weaker twin is scarcely registering, Mrs MacFarlane,' she murmured slowly. 'I've a daughter myself, so I know what you must be going through. But Mr Mapstone is one of the best ... Dorrie's in very good hands.'

Ailsa could only nod. Then she was left alone with her fears as Mr Mapstone and his staff strove to preserve the life of her unborn granddaughter.

'So I won't be home today, Josh,' Kirsty finished softly. She was sitting on the wide stairs at Chimneys, the telephone's wire laced through the carved balustrade. 'I'm sorry. I know you were planning something special for this evening.'

'Oh, no problem!' he assured her cheerfully, but he glanced disappointedly at the welcome-home bouquet of flowers, the Italian wine, and the carrier bag of fresh fruit and vegetables which he'd hastily dumped on the hall floor when he'd burst into the flat to answer the ringing phone. 'I'll cook you one of my fabulous dinners when you do get back!'

'I'll hold you to that!' Kirsty laughed wistfully. Although they talked every day and wrote long letters, these past weeks of separation had seemed an eternity. 'Mum didn't ask me if I could stay on here, she just sort of took it for granted. Besides, what else could I do? It'll only be for another day or two, I think … but I do miss you, Josh. I was counting the hours until–'

'Kirsty, don't!' He groaned. 'Or I'll be up in Yorkshire in a flash!'

'I wish!' she returned with feeling. 'Has my agent been in touch?' she added after a second or two. 'She does have my number here, but I thought perhaps she'd called the flat instead.'

'I don't know. She might have. I left for the studios around seven last night and I've only just got home,' he explained.

Kirsty had had a few lines in a popular soap earlier in the year, and now a new, regular character was to be introduced into the series, a part Kirsty was desperate to get. Her agent had been pressing for an audition.

'But people don't like being pressured,' Kirsty commented uneasily. 'Maybe I should have asked Ruth not to push too hard.'

'She wouldn't have paid any attention. Besides, she's right – you're talented, dedicated and you work harder than anyone else I know!' Josh declared loyally. 'Nobody deserves success more.'

'I know I'm lucky to be working regularly, and I do enjoy it – but I've had enough of walk-ons and bit parts and voice-overs and commercials!' she told him, a familiar frustration gnawing at her. 'I really need this. I want it so badly it's all I can think about!'

'I know,' Josh answered simply.

He'd shared the joys and exhilaration Kirsty sometimes experienced in her work, but he'd also held her close when she was feeling lost and defeated. He understood her, knew how vulnerable and insecure she really was. He loved her.

'You'll get the audition and the role,' he went on confidently. 'So when you do come back to me, we'll have a double celebration!'

'I'm–' She broke off at the almighty thudding coming from the room above. Robbie had been in a mood since the moment he'd opened his eyes that morning. It hardly seemed possible that a single, tiny person could create such chaos.

'Josh, I'll have to go, before Robbie and Teddy come through the ceiling!'

She discovered boy and dog tearing around the bedroom, leaping from one bed to another.

'Rob! I thought you were playing with your train set!' she exclaimed, glancing to the toybox with its strewn contents. 'Come on, let's take it out to the garden.'

Robbie trailed reluctantly downstairs.

'I want to go to playschool!' he protested for the umpteenth time.

'Robbie, I'm sorry,' she replied, lowering her voice as they passed by the sitting-room, where Alasdair was fast asleep on the couch, 'but if I take you to playschool, I'll have to leave Alasdair in the house alone, and I can't do that.'

'I'll go and wake–!'

'Oh, no you don't!' Kirsty chased after him, scooping him up under her arm as he was about to burst into the sitting-room.

'Phew – you little monkey!'

But Robbie didn't return her laugh. He wriggled and squirmed.

'Let me go! Put me down!' he cried, his face cross and flushed as he struggled. 'I want Mummy! Want my granny! I don't like you looking after me! I want to go to playschool. Why can't I go?'

'I've already explained,' Kirsty said patiently, bundling him into the kitchen. 'Look, why don't you tell me what you do at playschool? Maybe we can do it at home today.'

'Not the same.' He scowled, scuffing the floor with the toe of his sandals. 'We're making a castle. I got all my cornflakes boxes ready.'

'A castle, eh?' Kirsty hooked her thumbs into the belt of her shorts and knelt down beside the boy, who glared at her mutinously. 'I reckon we could make a pretty good castle–'

But Robbie was no longer listening. Hearing a familiar sound, he pushed past her, tore out into the garden and around the far side of the house.

Kirsty sprinted after him, but she stopped in her tracks when she rounded the corner. Paul Ashworth's car was parked at the gate and Robbie was already in his godfather's arms, tearfully pouring out his troubles.

With Ailsa away, Kirsty had realised it was almost inevitable that she was bound to see Paul, but her apprehension was instantly dispelled when she met his eyes and found not a trace of hostility there. Had he really forgiven her for walking out on him to go back to London?

'Auntie Kirsty!' Robbie raced towards her, his face glowing. 'Paul's taking me to play-school! I'll get my castle stuff!'

'That's terrific!' Kirsty beamed at the child's delight, calling after him as he vanished into the house, 'Shout if you need any help!'

'Has there been any word from Castildoro?' Paul asked quietly, joining her on the steep path. 'Or from the Foreign Office?'

She shook her head. 'I called those numbers you gave Mum. They're going to phone back. The chap I spoke to was sympathetic but seemed no wiser than us.'

'What they say, and what they actually know, are sometimes very different,' Paul remarked, studying her face keenly. He had no need to ask how she was. The dark smudges beneath her eyes told their own story.

'I may work on a country newspaper now, but I still have several contacts at the

Foreign Office. I could try cutting through the red tape to get some answers, if you like.'

'Oh, would you?' she entreated. 'This not knowing is awful.'

'I'll see to it, then.'

He fell into step beside her and they started around to the garden door.

'How's Ailsa bearing up?' he asked after a moment.

'Oh, you know her – somehow she always copes no matter what life throws at her.' Kirsty smiled. 'Actually she's had to go back to Auchlanrick. My sister's not well.'

'I'm sorry to hear that,' he returned. 'Robbie was telling me that Alasdair's asleep and not gone to school. Is he ill, too?'

'No, but with one thing and another, he was awake all last night.'

'You've told the children?' he asked with concern.

'Only Alasdair. He found out accidentally,' she replied ruefully, leading the way indoors. 'As for Janey… It just seemed wiser to wait. Sit down, won't you?' she offered as he followed her into the untidy kitchen. 'I'm sorry the place is such a clutter. This morning's been pretty hectic.'

Hastily she collected the dirty breakfast

dishes, unwilling to recount the tussle she'd had just getting Janey out of bed, not to mention the row over her wanting to wear high heels to school.

Kirsty knew how Isobel felt about such things but she hadn't had the heart to insist. Instead, she'd found herself watching as the girl stormed out of the house, wobbling precariously.

'I haven't got around to clearing up yet,' she finished uncomfortably, collecting the jugs of milk and orange juice and pushing them into the fridge. 'Even I'm usually better organised than this!'

'There's nothing wrong with a house being homely,' Paul commented easily, nudging aside a panda and stack of colouring books so he could sit down. 'My place always looks so tidy you wouldn't think anybody actually lives there!'

Robbie thundered downstairs at that moment, dragging a gaily-coloured rucksack bulging with empty cartons, kitchen roll tubes and washing-up liquid bottles.

'That looks heavy!' Paul's serious expression relaxed as he smiled down at the little boy. 'I think I'd better carry it.' He glanced at Kirsty. 'Shouldn't he be taking fruit or milk or something for lunch?'

'Sorry!' She darted into the pantry. 'Won't keep you a minute!'

Paul was settling the boy into the rear seat when Kirsty joined them at the car and passed in a little lunchbox for the child.

'I'll make those telephone calls.' Paul slid in behind the wheel. 'And I'll come over so we can tell Janey together when she gets in from school.'

'Thanks!' Kirsty had to raise her voice above the starting engine. 'For taking Robbie – and for all your help.'

He turned the key again, and the vehicle fell silent.

'Kirsty – I feel part of this family. You must know I'll do anything I can to help Isobel and Douglas.' Paul met her eyes steadily. 'And everything I can to help you – and the children.'

'I am to blame for us remaining here for longer than is wise, Luis,' Señor Bernaldez reasoned quietly. He and his grandson were sitting with Sam Fraser at the edge of the makeshift camp the party had made beneath the shelter of the forest trees. 'We must go on!'

'You're not strong enough, Cesar,' Luis returned earnestly. 'You must rest.'

'No. You've heard the military aircraft flying over.' The elderly man glanced towards the wreckage which Sam and the others had tried to camouflage with branches. 'It is purely good fortune that the pilots haven't sighted our plane.'

'Cesar's right,' Sam put in mildly, entering their conversation. 'We're on borrowed time. We have to move.'

'All right, all right,' Luis conceded in resignation. 'But it's madness to try to get to the border. It must be almost a hundred miles through inhospitable country–' He broke off, lowering his voice so it wouldn't carry on the hot, still air to the rest of the party. 'Castildoro is only three or four days' walk from here. Cesar needs medical attention and–' He inclined his head in Angela Lennard's direction. '–so does the girl.'

'Angela's arm is on the mend. She'll be fine,' Sam remarked shortly, beginning to lose patience with the young man's arguing. 'All this talk is pointless, Luis. You know perfectly well that it's impossible for you to go back to Castildoro!'

'I'm not afraid!' he said fervently. 'I didn't want to run away!'

'You're a young man, Luis,' Cesar interrupted gently. 'Your pride and sense of honour are wounded – this I understand. However, you cannot return.'

'Neither can Cesar – or I,' Sam reminded him curtly. 'Ortega will be looking for us – you can bet on that!'

'Because you helped me escape...' Luis sounded bitter and full of remorse. He offered no further objections and Señor Bernaldez drew in a relieved breath.

'I think we might now rejoin the others, Sam.' He rose awkwardly and started towards the bank of the stream where the Blundells, Angela Lennard and Karl Fischer were gathered. The map which Sam had just given them was spread on the ground.

'If this is our exact position,' Douglas began immediately, indicating one of the crosses Sam had marked on the map, 'then we were miles off course. Why didn't you tell us?'

'You didn't need to know.' Sam shrugged dismissively. 'Anyhow, we weren't off course.'

'Well, we aren't where we were supposed to be!' Karl Fischer observed grimly. 'I think we deserve an explanation.'

There was silence. Señor Bernaldez cleared his throat politely.

'I asked Sam to change our destination. Cross the border at a different place.'

Angela stared from him to Sam. 'And you agreed? Without consulting us? But we hired you! Our arrangement was–'

'You hired me,' Sam cut in, 'to get you out of the country. I'll still keep my part of the bargain. The route I've marked is the shortest way to the safest border. It'll be tough,' he added tersely, 'but I know the country. We'll make it.'

'You lied to us,' Karl Fischer countered. 'Yet you expect us to place our lives in your hands again?'

'What choice do you have?' Sam returned coldly. 'You can't stay here!'

'No, but we aren't as far from Castildoro as we thought.' Douglas spoke calmly. 'We can go back there.'

'That would be stupid! Oh, for heavens' sake, I've had this argument once already today!' Sam exclaimed contemptuously, turning on his heel. 'Cesar, Luis and I are leaving for the border in an hour. Come – or not – as you please!'

While Sam made his preparations, Douglas and the others began talking, trying to reach a decision.

Douglas distrusted Sam Fraser, and listened carefully to everything Angie and Karl had to say. And all the time, his eyes and attention were fixed on his wife. She hadn't complained – Isobel rarely did – but unlike the rest of them, she wasn't acclimatised to the high temperatures or the energy-draining humidity. Even in the shade of the trees, the heat was punishing. Isobel was visibly losing weight, and Douglas knew she was suffering frequent headaches and bouts of sickness.

'What do you think, Izzie?' he asked softly, reaching for her hand. 'What do you want to do?'

Why had he brought her to this wretched country? She should be safe at home with their children.

'Like you, I don't distrust Sam – and goodness knows what's happening in Castildoro,' Isobel murmured after a moment. 'But I think I'd still prefer that to trekking off into the unknown.'

'Me, too!' Angela spoke up. 'My father was a geologist with an engineering company and we've lived all over South America,' she explained, 'so I've a fair idea of what sort of country lies between us and the border. It'll be pretty hard going. Whatever the risks, at least Castildoro is civilisation.'

'And we're all American and British citizens,' Karl commented briskly. 'General Ortega would never endanger our lives. I vote we go back.'

'We're agreed, then,' Douglas rose and helped Isobel to her feet. 'We'll start as soon as we're ready.'

A few minutes later Angela was in the plane, sorting through her belongings. Fresh water for drinking and washing hadn't been a problem up till now – clear, quick-flowing streams ribboned the forest fringe. But from now on they'd need to carry water with them, probably enough to last until they reached Castildoro.

Ruefully discarding her meticulously kept journals, Angela was packing only the absolute essentials into her holdall when Luis climbed up into the wreckage.

'Allow me to assist you,' he said in his rather stilted English.

'Thanks, but I can manage,' she replied without turning round. 'There isn't much.'

'Even so...' He took the fleece sweater she'd been clumsily trying to fold one-handed, re-folded it, and placed it in the holdall. 'Going back to Castildoro is a great mistake,' he announced.

'Is it?' she asked coolly. 'From what I overheard earlier, you wanted to go back!'

'I have – personal reasons.' He hesitated. 'My father is still in the city.'

'I see.' Angela continued sorting. 'I'm sorry.'

'Professor Fischer is naïve to imagine that, because you are American citizens, you will be safe,' Luis persisted. 'I am familiar with General Ortega. He is a ruthless man. Your country's flag will offer no protection.

'Despite what you think, Sam Fraser is a good man. A good friend. You must come with us!' he concluded, reaching out to touch her arm. 'Miss Lennard – Angela – there is danger in Castildoro. Please – believe me!'

'How can I?' Angela challenged, moving away from his touch. 'Neither you nor Sam nor your grandfather have been honest with us!'

'I'm not sure I–' he faltered.

'Oh, don't try to deny it!' she exclaimed. 'When you and Señor Bernaldez boarded the plane, Sam pretended you were strangers – but you know each other very well, don't you? And you were supposed to be just passing through Castildoro. But nobody "just passes through" Castildoro!

'And you're certainly not a medical student, as your grandfather said – if that old man *is* your grandfather, which I'm seriously starting to doubt! I like you, and I'd like to believe you, but I just can't.

'Luis – oh, Luis!' She broke off with a despairing shake of her head. 'You've only ever told us your first name, haven't you? Is even that genuine?'

He sat across the aisle from where she was standing, staring up into her flushed, accusing face for a long moment. Then he gave a kind of shrug.

'I'm ashamed to admit you are correct about almost everything. I've known Sam Fraser most of my life – he's flown frequently for my father. Cesar and I aren't related, but he's an old and trusted family friend,' he confided frankly. 'And I care for him deeply. And you're right to suspect that I'm not studying medicine,' he finished with another shrug. 'I'm doing post-graduate history at university in Los Angeles. My younger sister studies there, also. Fortunately my mother was visiting her when the troubles started, so they are both safe.'

'And is that where you're heading?' Angela asked, her curiosity getting the better of her. 'Los Angeles?'

'Eventually.' He linked his fingers loosely, hesitating again before continuing. 'But my name *is* Luis, Angela – Luis Rosales.'

'Rosales?' she echoed, a sudden awareness leaping into her eyes. 'You're – the son of

President Rosales?'

'Yes. While my father remains in our country to fight–' His words fractured emotionally. '–I go to join my mother and sister!'

'I can understand how you feel,' Angela ventured, 'but if you'd stayed, you might have endangered your father. If you were captured by Ortega's troops, you'd be a valuable hostage.'

'My father said precisely that to persuade me to leave.' He smiled grimly. 'But it's no consolation, I can assure you. And I will return – but you cannot, Angela!'

'What you've told me certainly explains a lot – but it doesn't alter the situation for the rest of us,' she answered slowly, touched by the genuine concern in his dark eyes. 'We have to go back to Castildoro!'

Chapter Five

Her Heart's Desire

Kirsty had pushed aside the sitting-room furniture and was working out to one of her aerobics tapes when the call from Ruth Hartman finally came.

The theatrical agent had scarcely hung up before Kirsty was excitedly dialling Josh's number. Not since her mid-teens had anybody believed in her as Josh did and she was impatient to share her happiness with him.

'I've got the audition!' she cried the instant he picked up the phone.

'Fantastic! I knew you would!'

'I'm to read on Monday!' Kirsty explained, elation bubbling up inside her. After so many years of struggling and dreaming and being disappointed, suddenly – incredibly – everything she'd been working for was at last within reach.

'According to Ruth, two of the directors saw me in that play at Bristol and really liked my work and she reckons I've a good chance of getting the role. Oh, if only I do… Imagine – me, on television twice a week – maybe for years. I can hardly believe it!'

'Well, I can. And I'd give anything for us to be together right now!'

'Mmm … me, too!' She laughed. 'Mum's back tomorrow, so I'll be home for that dinner you promised. I can't wait to see you again!'

Calling Ailsa and telling her the great news was next on the agenda. However, there was no answer from the house at Auchlanrick so Kirsty resumed her work-out, resolving to try again later. The phone rang just a few minutes later, though, and she scrambled to answer it.

'Josh? Oh, Mum!' Kirsty was delighted. 'I'm so glad you've called. I've been trying to ring you!'

'I'm not at home,' Ailsa began. 'I'm–'

'Hang on – I can't hear properly. I'll just turn off the music.'

'All right.' Ailsa sighed wearily.

She was using the pay-phone in the corridor close to Dorrie's room. She'd scarcely left the hospital for what seemed like days, spending hours beside Dorrie's bedside, or sitting in the hospital chapel.

Thankfully, the crisis had passed. The

scanner's indistinct images of their babies, living and moving, had offered hope to Dorrie and Graham as nothing else could have done.

Hope sometimes wasn't enough, though, and Mr Mapstone had been realistic when he'd answered Ailsa's blunt questions...

'That's better!' Kirsty was back on the line. 'Mum, you'll never guess – I'm up for a part in a new TV soap! My audition's on Monday. Ruth's already got the script and my character's from Rochdale, so I'll have to really work on the accent. I'm going to study recordings of some of Gracie Fields's interviews to get the speech rhythms–'

She paused, suddenly aware that Ailsa hadn't responded to her news at all.

'Mum? Are you still there?'

'I'm still here,' Ailsa replied shortly. 'I dare say it's all very thrilling for you, but I'm wondering if you're even going to ask after your sister!'

'Sorry! My head's in the clouds.' Kirsty could have kicked herself for her thought-lessness. 'How is Dorrie?'

'Her condition's stabilised – but she's still very ill – and she might still lose the babies. The doctor was perfectly frank about that. The wee girl is especially at risk.'

Ailsa swallowed the knot in her throat and kept her voice even.

'I'm not leaving Dorrie. She needs me. You'll be all right coping with the children for a few days more, won't you?'

'No! I can't stay any longer, Mum! I have to go back to London tomorrow. Josh and I are having a special dinner together. And I'm auditioning on Monday!'

'Yes, so you've told me.' Ailsa's voice was sharp. 'All you think about these days is yourself and this part and that part. You don't seem to care about your family any more. If this is what being an actress is doing to you – well, it's high time you grew up and saw sense! There are far more important things in life than gadding about with your boyfriend and prancing about on stage. I didn't want you to take it up in the first place. It's nothing but a waste of time!'

Kirsty was stunned.

'That's not fair!' she cried, stung into retaliation. 'Josh is special – and acting's my job! It means a lot to me – why must you constantly ridicule it? But then, you've never understood. It was only Dad and Granny MacFarlane who encouraged me. You've never cared about me as much as Isobel and Dorrie,' she went on bitterly. 'I accepted that

100

long ago. But I'm still your daughter! I know I haven't done what you expected of me – getting married and having children – but doesn't it matter whether I'm happy or not?'

'This isn't–' Ailsa cut in, but Kirsty's emotions were boiling over and she couldn't stop.

'Nothing – nobody – is going to stop me going to that audition!' she concluded, breathless and trembling as she moved to slam down the phone. 'This is the opportunity of a lifetime. Come what may, I'm taking it!'

The crash of her slamming down the telephone receiver ended their conversation, but even as her trembling fingers were uncurling from the instrument, the appalling realisation of what she'd done – what she'd said – hit her. When would she ever learn to think before she spoke?

Clumsy in her haste, she dialled the house at Auchlanrick, waiting impatiently while the phone rang and rang. Why on earth didn't her mother answer?

But, of course, she'd been calling from the hospital! There was no way of reaching her. No way of explaining, of making amends…

She shivered, chilling rapidly after her work-out, and started upstairs for a hot shower. She'd have to call Josh, too. Let him know she wouldn't be home tomorrow after all.

She halted on the landing, hearing Janey's angry shouting and Alasdair's usually quiet voice raised above the blaring television below.

Racing downstairs again, she burst into the kitchen. Alasdair was sitting at the large table, surrounded by his books, while Janey was standing in the middle of the floor, hands on hips, her face white with anger.

The portable television was at full volume while the tap was gushing steaming water into the sink. Brother and sister were arguing so furiously they weren't even aware that Kirsty had entered.

'Quiet!' she bellowed. 'What's going on?'

'He won't–'

'Look what she's–'

They both began at once until Kirsty held up a hand to silence them.

'One at a time, for goodness' sake! Now, who was in here first?' she demanded, snapping off the television and turning off the water. 'Alasdair–?'

'That's not fair!' Janey protested but Kirsty fixed her with a look that silenced her.

'You'll have your turn in a minute, Janey. Now, Alasdair – what's happened?'

The boy flushed, lowering his eyes and remaining silent.

'I asked you a question!' she bellowed again, and he looked up.

'I wanted Janey to turn down the TV because I was doing my homework,' he mumbled uncomfortably, fiddling with the corner of an atlas. 'But she turned it up louder instead.'

'It's my favourite programme!' Janey was unable to hold her tongue a second longer. 'I want to watch it!'

'You weren't watching it!' he retorted accusingly. 'You were messing about at the sink!'

'I'm washing my skating skirt! And you shouldn't be in here, anyhow. Why don't you go to your room?'

'Robbie's painting. I don't want him to splash my books!'

'Why not go into the sitting-room then?'

'That's enough!' Kirsty's voice was sharp. 'I was working out in there and I haven't put the furniture back yet.'

'I'll help you,' Janey returned, adding rudely, 'Then he can go in – and stay in!'

'I untidied it – so I'll tidy it!' Kirsty said

firmly. 'But I must change first. Meanwhile – would you like to work in the study, Alasdair?'

He nodded eagerly and started to gather his books together. His father's study was his favourite room in the whole house but usually nobody was allowed in there.

'After I finish my maths, I'm going to draw a big map of Castildoro. I want to mark where Paul told us the plane landed.' He hesitated, glancing at Kirsty. 'I thought, once they found the plane, Mum and Dad would be coming home–?'

'Can't you shut up about that?' Janey's grey eyes were glinting. 'You bore everyone stiff with what you've read about Castildoro. Can't you understand that there's no point? Mum and Dad'll be home soon. What good will your stupid map be then?'

Alasdair flinched as though she'd slapped him, but didn't reply. Janey turned pointedly to Kirsty.

'Aunt Kirsty, do you think this coffee stain will wash out? I need my skirt for tonight.'

'Are you going skating this evening?' Kirsty asked in concern, examining the dark splash on the short, full skirt. 'Is Paul driving you? No? Then I don't think you ought to go.'

'But I've already told Amanda!' her niece retorted, her eyes narrowing.

Kirsty shook her head. 'It'll be after dark when you come home on the bus. Besides, you've school tomorrow.'

'I won't be late. I promise,' Janey insisted. 'And Amanda's brother will bring us back in his car. Marcus is eighteen and he's just started working at the rink's coffee bar.'

'So that's why you've been hanging around there and at the Braithwaite farm,' Alasdair commented matter-of-factly, scraping back his chair. 'You want Marcus Braithwaite to take you to the school dance.'

Janey's mouth dropped open, her cheeks flamed. 'You horrible little–!'

Alasdair was already turning into the hall but as Janey made to go after him Kirsty raised a hand.

'Let it be,' she advised. 'Give me a moment to change, then we'll tackle that stain.'

'Then it's all right?' Janey asked cautiously, her expression brightening. 'Thanks! I told Amanda you wouldn't say no!'

It wasn't until Janey had dashed off to the Braithwaite farm to meet Amanda, and Robbie had finally tired himself out and fallen asleep, that Kirsty found a quiet moment to ring Auchlanrick again.

'Mum – I'm sorry about earlier,' she began quietly. 'Of course you must be with Dorrie. And don't worry about things here. We'll be fine.'

'I'm sure you will!' Ailsa's response was warm. 'I knew you'd do the right thing when you'd calmed down. After all, you haven't any ties of your own in London, have you?'

They talked for a few minutes longer, then Kirsty rang off and wandered out into the warm, dusky garden. Leaning a shoulder against the honeysuckle-soaked trellis, she gazed out at the silent moors and purple-shadowed hills.

Staying at Chimneys meant being away from Josh, and thinking of him filled her with sharp, aching loneliness.

'You look bright-eyed and bushy-tailed,' Kirsty remarked next morning when Janey was first down for breakfast. 'Considering the hour you sneaked in last night!'

Janey grinned sheepishly. 'I did say I was sorry for keeping you up. And it wasn't that late.'

Kirsty raised an eyebrow, and stooped to gather the post. Her agent had express-mailed the audition script, there was a post-card from the optician in Cottingby, and several letters for Isobel.

'You should try to get home earlier, all the same,' Kirsty remarked thoughtfully, wondering if she should start opening Isobel's mail. Douglas's too. There would be bills, all kinds of household matters needing attention. 'Especially during the week.'

'All right.' The girl beamed, her eyes sparkling. 'Oh, I'll burst if I don't tell someone!' She lowered her voice, even though Mrs Bell was in the pantry and out of hearing. 'Marcus is going to ask me to the dance! I just know he is!'

'Can he?' Kirsty inquired.

'What? Oh, I see. Partners don't have to be from school,' Janey explained. 'It's a huge occasion, you know. There're fifth and sixth formers from other schools beside ours, so hundreds go. It's held in the ballroom at Cottingby Town Hall with a proper band and a buffet and everything!'

'Is this your first dance?'

Janey nodded. 'First adult one,' she agreed, then confided cheerfully, 'I was dreading it! The other girls already have partners, you see. And five boys – *five* – asked Amanda! I was scared I'd be the only one without a boy to go with. Now I've got Marcus. I can't wait!'

'Marcus Braithwaite?' Winifred Bell emerged from the pantry with a bucket and mop. 'I've seen – *heard* – him roaring through the village in that rusty old car of his.'

'Marcus is very proud of his car, Mrs Bell,' Janey exclaimed, putting on her blazer. 'He was telling me about it. It's a classic model.'

Winifred sniffed. 'And I'm a Dutchman!' She turned her attention to the mail which Kirsty had left on the dresser. 'Robbie's specs are ready to be collected from the optician, eh? That was quick!'

'Mmm, we'll pop into Cottingby after lunch and collect – Janey!' Kirsty broke off, glancing around as the teenager grabbed her bag and made off along the hall. 'What about breakfast?'

'No time! I'm meeting Amanda. We want to get the early bus and window-shop for dresses.'

'Hard to credit I was like that once,' Mrs Bell commented to Kirsty as the back door clattered shut. 'Have you got anything sorted for your audition?'

'No.' She sighed, regretfully eyeing the bulky script on the dresser. 'I'm desperate to do it, but it would mean I was away until evening. With the children to consider…'

Mrs Bell looked thoughtful.

'After I bring Harry back from his physio, I can hold the fort here for a few hours. And why don't you have a word with Kate Wakefield?' she suggested, adding, when Kirsty clearly didn't recognise the name, 'Tall and thin with red hair? Runs the playschool?'

'Oh, of course! The minister's daughter. Paul introduced us.' Kirsty nodded. 'D'you really think she'd help?'

'She'd be glad to. Kate's a grand young lass.' Winifred was fetching polish and dusters from the cupboard. 'Why, between the three of us, we'll have you on the telly yet!'

Although the visit to the optician was quickly over, Robbie was distinctly subdued when they got outside, fidgeting with the unfamiliar little spectacles.

'Fancy going for a milk shake?' Kirsty suggested, as they started along Cottingby's High Street.

Robbie just sighed, and shook his head dolefully.

'How about ice-cream then?' she persisted, hoping to cheer him up. 'A great big one, with chocolatey bits?'

He shook his head again, staring at his sandals.

'Want to go home.'

'You're the boss!' Kirsty smiled, taking his hand and crossing towards her car. 'Let's go home!'

Even as she unlocked the kitchen door and Teddy came, tail wagging, to greet them, Kirsty heard Janey and Amanda's voices. She glanced at the clock. What were they doing here at this time when they should still be at school? Bunking off to talk about boys, no doubt. Then she caught the unmistakable smell of cigarettes...

'Kirsty!' Janey jerked round, startled and guilty-looking as her aunt flung open the door and strode into the sitting-room. 'I – I didn't think you'd be back so–'

'Evidently!' Kirsty snapped, taking in the cola cans, crisp bags, fashion magazines and ashtray littering the carpet where the girls were sprawled. 'Have you lost your mind? Don't you realise how dangerous smoking is?'

She bent to scoop up the cigarette packet and a cheap lighter and rounded on Amanda.

'Are these yours? Take them – and get out!'

Sullen-faced, the girl snatched them from

Kirsty's hand and grabbed her school blazer from where it was draped over a chair. As she sauntered from the room, she turned to Janey.

'See you tonight at the rink?'

'Definitely!'

'No–' Kirsty interrupted curtly. 'Janey won't be there tonight. And don't come here again, Amanda. You're not welcome!'

The girl shrugged and stalked out of the room.

'How dare you!' Janey hissed at Kirsty the instant her friend had gone. 'How dare you humiliate me like that!' She was so furious she could scarcely get the words out. 'You've no right to order me and my friends about. No right!'

'Janey, wait–' Kirsty began, but the girl pushed past her, then paused at the doorway to glare at her with open hostility.

'This isn't your house, Aunt Kirsty,' she ground out, 'and you're not my mother!' She hadn't cried at the news of her parents' disappearance but now tears of rage and resentment glittered in her eyes. 'We don't even want you here. So why don't you just go back to London and leave us alone!'

The waterhole in the forest hollow was the

first they'd come across since parting from Sam Fraser and the others. Although they didn't dare risk drinking the brackish water, it was adequate for washing – just.

'I'm not sure what I'm looking forward to most,' Angela remarked wryly to Isobel, wringing out her cotton shirt. 'Shampooing my hair, taking a proper bath in clean, hot water – or having a cup of coffee! After this, I'll never grumble about the Castildoro hotel ever again.'

'At least we'll look clean and halfway decent when we arrive,' Isobel observed thoughtfully, using her fingers to tease the tangles from her wet hair.

By unspoken agreement, during their days of walking nobody had speculated upon the fate awaiting them in Castildoro.

They'd become accustomed to the night skies being alive with military aircraft, but this morning they'd seen planes flying in daylight for the first time. And now they were close enough to the capital city to hear muffled explosions and bursts of gunfire.

The agitated shrieking of monkeys high in the dense canopy of trees warned of yet more planes approaching. Despite the steamy heat, Isobel was suddenly cold.

Clambering from the shallows, she sat on

the baked mud surrounding the waterhole. It was covered with paw marks – splayed reptilian claws, slender hooves and the large, flat paw-marks of wild cats.

Isobel purposefully took an address book from her pocket and concentrated on sketching the tracks.

The notebook and pencil had been a Mother's Day gift from Janey and the boys. She had been unable to part with it when she'd left her other belongings behind.

'Are you keeping a diary?' Angela asked with interest, joining her on the bank.

Isobel shook her head. 'It's sort of a letter for my children. I jot down how clear the stars are ... describe the wonderfully coloured birds ... how much like Robinson Crusoe Douglas looks now he can't shave... Just silly wee things, but...' She smiled self-consciously. 'Somehow, while I'm writing, it's like I'm talking to them.'

'You've two boys and a girl, haven't you?' Angela asked, offering her the tin mug of paste she'd ground together from barks, leaves and tuberous roots. They'd used up their supply of insect repellent, and although this old Indian remedy had an unpleasantly sweet odour, it did soothe the burning, itching bites.

'I've seen the children's photograph – yours, too – in Douglas's tent at the dig,' Angela went on.

Isobel sighed. 'I keep imagining them expecting me home last Tuesday,' she murmured sadly, a faraway expression in her eyes. 'They would have been waiting and waiting, but I never came. They'll be feeling so lost and afraid.'

Angela tried to smile encouragingly. 'It might be possible for us to make a telephone call when we get into town – or mail a letter, at least.'

'What will it be like?' Isobel asked suddenly. 'You understand this country. What'll happen to us?'

Angela gave a resigned shrug and got to her feet.

'My guess isn't any better than anybody else's. Political unrest can rumble on for years down here and then suddenly explode. Often it's over as swiftly as it began and life goes on pretty much as before,' she continued, as they clambered up the slope to rejoin Douglas and Karl. 'Despite the military activity, the situation in Castildoro might not be as bad as we fear. But whatever the situation, we do have to return,' she concluded practically. 'We've no place else to go.'

They were about an hour from the city limits, following a track cut between forest and cane fields, when the roar of aircraft drew nearer and passed directly overhead, flying low.

Isobel looked up, getting her first proper sight of the planes. They appeared curiously old fashioned.

She instinctively pushed her fingers into Douglas's clenched hand. He didn't turn to her. His face was raised, his eyes narrowed as he watched the planes flying towards Castildoro.

Isobel looked away. If the city was about to be bombed, she didn't want to see it.

'Must be more than a hundred–' Karl broke off, hastily adjusting the lens on his binoculars. 'They're dropping parachutists!'

Douglas took the glasses and scanned the area.

'Not on the city. The far side of it!' he announced.

Isobel turned back in time to see the great mass of planes disappearing beyond the distant saw-toothed foothills.

When they started walking again, they moved more cautiously than ever, and when they came to a blind corner, Douglas edged on alone, threading through the trees.

'The track's blocked by a Jeep and half a dozen soldiers,' he told Isobel and the others when he stole back a few minutes later. 'There's no way we'll get by without being challenged. And they're heavily armed.'

Isobel moved closer to him and Douglas put his arm about her shoulders. From the look in his eyes, she knew he was blaming himself again for bringing her to Castildoro.

She raised her chin defiantly, desperate to reassure him. She mustn't let him sense how scared she was.

'Aren't there other roads into the city?' she asked. 'Smaller ones – that might not be guarded?'

Douglas nodded. 'If Karl and I get on to that ridge–' He shielded his eyes, pointing to the high ground above the rows and rows of tall sugar cane. '–we can work our way down through the fields and get close enough to see exactly what's going on in the city. Then we'll know if we've got a chance of reaching the hotel.'

'I want you to stay here, Isobel.' He glanced quickly at Angela. 'Both of you. Keep well out of sight and–'

'Where you go, I go!' Isobel interrupted quietly. 'We agreed not to be separated.'

'It makes no sense for Isobel and me to

hang around here,' Angela chipped in, using her shirt sleeve to rub the perspiration trickling into her eyes. 'We could be picked up at any time. Let's just get started.'

It was a hard climb to the ridge, with the midday sun beating relentlessly down. Isobel's legs were leaden, her heart pounding, as Douglas hauled her up the final yards. She found herself on a stony ledge, high over the canes, which offered a good view of Castildoro.

'Keep down,' Karl warned, inching forward on his stomach. He propped his elbows on the ground and adjusted the binoculars before sweeping the ground below.

'What—?' Angela began in a low voice, but Douglas instantly raised a forefinger to his lips. Following his gesture downwards, they saw a solitary soldier patrolling the field perimeter close to a machine store. No more than seventeen or eighteen years old, the boy was wearing the dull green battle-dress of General Ortega's army and an automatic weapon was slung carelessly over his shoulder.

Wordlessly the binoculars were passed from one to another. When Isobel's turn came, her hands were trembling so much that Douglas had to steady the glasses for her.

Controlling the panic rising within her, Isobel stared down into Castildoro.

The streets were empty of people. No old men gathered beneath the shady awnings outside the cantina, dozing away the afternoon or playing checkers. No children racing through the dusty streets or selling fruit and ice from the corners. No women drawing water from the pump in the square.

Instead there were soldiers everywhere. They sauntered around the deserted streets and stood outside the bank, police station and post office. They were stationed behind barricades of sandbags high on the flat rooftops of the public and government buildings. And all of them looked as young as the boy in the cane field.

Fearing they would be spotted at any second, Isobel was anxious to get away from the ledge as quickly as possible. But descending the ridge again, her chest was so constricted with fear that she could scarcely breathe. She was terrified that the crack of a twig, or the rattle of a loose rock would alert the sentry in the cane field.

Not until they were safely across the guarded track and amongst the forest trees did any of them breathe easily. It was Angela who spoke first.

'We haven't got a drop of fresh water left – and hardly any food. We can't get down into Castildoro now – so what do we do?'

'The dig,' Karl said simply. 'It's our only hope.'

'That's another six or seven hours of hard walking away,' Douglas commented, his eyes fleetingly upon Isobel.

'We could make it before nightfall,' Angela pressed, looking to Isobel for support. 'The site's well equipped. We'll have food, water, vehicles. Even radio – if we're lucky.'

'And if the rest of the team are still working there, we'll be able to link up with them and make our plans accordingly,' Karl put in.

With the shock subsiding, Isobel felt drained in mind as well as body. But she knew Angela and Karl were right. She met Douglas's anxious eyes and nodded positively.

'I think we ought to keep going.'

The sun was dipping gold and red at the horizon when Isobel and the others stumbled wearily into the site of the archaeological excavation. None of Douglas's team were there. And it looked as if they hadn't been there for some time.

The poles and ropes dividing the grids were flattened and strewn across the sandy ground, benches were overturned and books, trays and equipment tossed aside. Angela's old station-wagon and a Jeep were bogged down into the soft earth.

In the gathering gloom of evening, the four wandered amongst the looted tents and huts, assessing what was left.

'Whoever did this was in a hurry. They only stole what they could easily carry – which means we're in luck,' Karl remarked ironically, emerging from one of the sheds. 'The radio and transmitter are still here.'

Suddenly brilliant light flooded the darkness, pinning them in its dazzling beam. Isobel glimpsed the dull green of a military uniform behind the light and tried to get to Douglas's side.

A harsh voice froze her where she stood.

'Don't move.' The command was chillingly quiet and very, very near. 'Any of you!'

Chapter Six

'It's All Going Wrong!'

'That was a fine sermon, George,' Paul Ashworth was saying to the Reverend Wakefield as he and Kirsty shepherded the children from the village church after Sunday services. 'I'm sorry one of us dropped a handful of marbles!'

'Don't worry about it. It's difficult sitting still when the sun's shining and you'd much rather be outside,' the elderly minister replied philosophically. 'Eh, Robbie?'

'Yes,' the boy agreed readily, then looked up at Kirsty with an appealing smile. 'Can I go and ride my bike now?'

'Off you go!'

As Robbie sped off, Reverend Wakefield turned to Kirsty.

'Miss Macfarlane, I understand from my daughter that you're to stay on in Ferneys Beck?'

Kirsty smiled. 'For a while,' she agreed.

'It goes without saying that we're keeping

you all in our prayers at this time,' the minister continued. 'But if there's anything Kate or I can do – anything at all – please don't hesitate to ask.'

'That's very kind, Mr Wakefield,' she returned warmly. 'Actually Kate's been a wonderful help already.'

'What was that all about?' Paul asked curiously as they started down the wide path beneath the arching yews of the church grounds. 'I didn't realise you knew Kate Wakefield.'

'Got you guessing, hasn't it?' Kirsty chuckled. 'Thanks to Kate and Mrs Bell, I'm going to Manchester tomorrow!'

'Ah, yes, your audition,' Paul murmured reflectively, falling into step beside her as they passed through the high church gates.

Kirsty had been very young when he'd first met her at Isobel and Douglas's wedding but romance hadn't exactly blossomed between bridesmaid and best man. Oh, they'd seen each other occasionally at Christmases and christenings and had even occasionally gone out for lunch or dinner; but it wasn't until two summers ago that their easy-going friendship had unexpectedly changed for ever.

Kirsty had turned up at Chimneys for one of her spur-of-the-moment holidays and they'd found themselves spending almost every day and evening together. At some point, Paul had fallen in love, confident that Kirsty felt the same.

Then the call from her agent had come – and within a couple of hours, Kirsty had gone just as suddenly as she'd arrived.

Paul had followed her, told her he loved her, asked her to come back to Yorkshire with him. But Kirsty had put her career first and turned him down. She always put her career first – he'd learned that the hard way.

He took a steadying breath, surprised at how much it hurt to remember her rejection and their bitter quarrel. He glanced at her. She was laughing, carefree, waving wildly to Robbie as he and two other toddlers pedalled furiously around the green on their trikes.

'Do you think you'll get the part?' he asked rather brusquely.

'There's some as thinks I will, chuck!' She grinned, slipping easily into the broad accent she'd spent hours perfecting. 'And if I don't, it won't be for the lack of trying – or wishing. I want it so badly, I–'

'Auntie Kirsty!' Robbie was wobbling by. 'Can Joe and Penny come to our picnic?'

'If their mums say it's OK,' Kirsty replied cheerfully. 'The more the merrier!'

Paul got a grip on his thoughts.

'A picnic instead of traditional Sunday lunch was a good idea,' he commented.

'Hmm – well, Izzie always makes Sunday such a family occasion. I thought if I tried to do the same, it'd just make her absence all the worse,' Kirsty answered soberly. 'Obviously, the children are missing them both terribly – and this being the first Sunday she should have been home–'

'Paul! Kirsty!' Kate Wakefield called to them from the church gates and came scurrying along the lane after them. 'Robbie's glasses! I found them amongst the hymn books. He must've dropped them.'

'Thanks, Kate! He keeps taking them off and leaving them all over the place.' Kirsty shook her head in light-hearted exasperation. 'I hadn't even noticed he wasn't wearing them.'

Kate returned her smile. 'Small children often take a while to adjust to specs,' she reassured her. 'He'll settle into them soon enough and forget he's wearing them. Oh, by the way – bring him to the parsonage as early as you like tomorrow. I have several little ones whose parents drop them off before going to work, so we open our doors at breakfast-time! And if I don't happen to see you,' she concluded brightly, 'break a leg! Isn't that what they say?'

She strode off briskly, then paused at the church gates to look back over her shoulder at Paul.

A tall man, his dark head was inclined towards the much smaller Kirsty as they strolled along together, chatting and laughing as Robbie pedalled between them. Acting together, they each took hold of a handgrip, giving the trike a helpful pull over a bumpy patch...

Kate sighed wistfully and turned away, hurrying through the gates and up into the empty church.

Though it was long past midnight, Kirsty was wide awake. She'd lit a fire in the sitting-room and was stretched out on the window-seat studying her script. She already knew it, but...

A gentle tapping on the window and a face grinning at her through the glass had her flying into the hall and pulling open the front door.

'Josh!' she exclaimed in astonishment, virtually falling into his open arms. 'Oh,

Josh! What are you doing here?'

'Soon as I finished at the studio, I hit the road! This is going to be an important day for you, sweetheart, and I want to be part of it.' He held her tightly for a moment.

'I thought you might need some moral support, too,' he went on as she drew him indoors.

'Oh, people have been really helpful,' she replied enthusiastically, raising her face for another kiss. 'Oh, Josh – I can't believe you're really here!'

'Auntie Kirsty...?' A thin, sleepy voice drifted down the stairs.

She grinned ruefully, moving out of Josh's embrace.

'That's Robbie. I'll have to see what he wants. Back in a second – stay right where you are!'

However, when she came downstairs again, Josh wasn't where she'd left him. She found him in the kitchen, standing at the stove with his back to her. He had discarded his jacket and pushed his shirt sleeves up over his fore-arms. There was a cardboard box on the table that hadn't been there earlier.

She paused in the doorway, watching him. She loved watched him like this. His move-ments had an easy economy, with none of the flashiness some men displayed when they were cooking and hoping to impress.

Sensing her presence, he glanced round and smiled.

'Hi. I didn't hear you come down. How long have you been standing there?'

'A while,' she admitted, and crossed the room, slipping her arms around his waist and resting her cheek between his shoulder blades. 'I like watching you cook.'

Josh laughed quietly. 'You mean you like watching me do all the work!'

Kirsty stood on tiptoe, touching her lips to his ear.

'What are you making anyway?'

'Pizza, of course! I'm half Italian – what else would I cook at two-thirty in the morning?'

'It smells great!' she remarked appreciatively. 'I hope it doesn't waken the children and bring them down.'

Josh stretched out a hand and closed the kitchen door firmly.

'Problem solved! I brought a few other things in the car,' he went on, going to the cardboard box. 'The wine's already chilling, and these are for you.'

'Freesias! My favourites! Thank you!' She buried her face into the fragrant petals, laughing as he darted back to rescue a saucepan.

'I'll just put these in water then set the sitting-room table,' she announced. 'I'm sure Isobel has some fancy candles tucked away somewhere.'

The pizza was soon ready, and after they had eaten, they took their wine to the fireside rug. Kirsty curled up next to Josh, her head against his chest.

'After that drive, you must be exhausted,' she murmured at length. 'I'll fix up the spare room.'

'Don't bother.' He stretched contentedly. 'I'll be OK down here. But you should get some sleep.'

'Wouldn't be able to.' She nestled closer. 'Besides, I don't want to be away from you for even a second!'

Early sunshine was flooding the room when Kirsty opened her eyes. Josh's jacket was draped over her and he was smiling down at her, holding out a tall glass of orange juice.

'I let you sleep as long as possible, but...' He shrugged apologetically.

She came wide awake with a jolt, elbowing herself up against the couch cushions. 'What time is it? What–?'

'Take it easy! The housekeeper – Mrs Bell, isn't it? – came and sorted out the kids. They've gone, and so has she. Everything's under control.'

'Winifred's terrific,' Kirsty said thankfully, butterflies starting to flutter in her stomach as she thought ahead several hours. 'Josh, what do you think of my hair?'

'I love it.' He smoothed his fingertips through the soft waves, fanning them about her shoulders. 'I told you that last night.'

'Mmm, so you did.' She smiled, remembering. 'Actually, I meant for my character. Should I pin it up? Wear lots of colourful slides?'

'If it helps create the illusion – why not?' He followed her from the room, glancing at his watch. 'But don't take too long. We'll have to leave soon.'

She was racing to where Josh was waiting in the hall when the telephone rang.

He grasped her wrist as she reached for it. 'Leave it! We haven't time.'

'I can't! Suppose it's Mum? Or Isobel, even?'

He agreed, but warily, knowing what Kirsty was like once she got on the phone.

'I'll bring the car round,' he told her warningly.

When she slid into the passenger seat a few minutes later, she was frowning anxiously.

'It was Kate Wakefield at the playschool,' she explained. 'Robbie's had a bit of a fight with a bigger boy. Kate said neither one is hurt, but Robbie's upset. His nose has been bleeding.' She shook her head in disbelief. 'They're hardly more than toddlers!'

'It probably isn't nearly so alarming as it sounds,' Josh reassured her, briefly touching her cheek before he started the car. 'Small boys do have fights. And nose-bleeds and bruises and skinned knees!'

She shrugged. 'Even so – Kate said he was crying. Wanting his mum.'

She was thoughtful as they approached the village.

'Josh – stop! That's the parsonage over there. I could just pop in and check Robbie's OK.' She hastily unbuckled her seat-belt. 'Won't be a minute!'

'I'll wait here.' Josh checked his watch as she got out. 'But be quick!'

Kirsty sprinted over the gravelled driveway and up the stone steps into the double-fronted Georgian parsonage. Pausing in the parquet hall she tried to get her bearings.

'In here!' Kate Wakefield called cheerfully

from a gaily decorated room to Kirsty's left. 'We're playing a rhyming game!'

Kirsty whirled around and saw Robbie scrambling from Kate's lap and making a beeline towards her.

'Auntie Kirsty!'

He wasn't crying now, but his eyes were red-rimmed and swollen, and his flushed cheeks streaked with dried tears.

'What is it, darling?' she whispered, bending to pick him up. 'What's wrong?'

Robbie flung his chubby arms about her and Kirsty dropped to her knees, holding him tight.

'Auntie Kirsty,' he mumbled, burrowing his face into her neck. 'Want to go home!'

'Shh, it's all right,' she comforted him, scarcely recognising a sudden surge of unfamiliar tenderness as he cuddled into her. 'I'm here...'

'Kirsty!' Josh's voice came from behind her. 'We've got to go – now!'

As Robbie whimpered, clutching fearfully at her, Kirsty tightened her grasp on him.

'He needs me, Josh,' she answered softly, wonderingly, without looking up. 'I can't go away and leave him. I can't!'

'Kirsty! They'll not give you another audition,' Josh warned in a low voice, watching her cuddle the child. 'It's now or never. You don't have any choice!'

'Yes, I do,' she answered simply.

Beaming reassuringly at Robbie, she set him down in front of her, her hands lingering on his shoulders.

'Is there anything you need to bring home with you? Then off you go and fetch it.'

He turned, taking half a dozen steps before stopping and trotting back to her. He curled his small fingers around hers anxiously.

'You won't go away?' the boy implored, raising his face to hers. 'Please, Auntie Kirsty?'

'No, I won't go away, I promise!' she murmured, her voice catching. 'Now get your stuff!'

His feet thumped on the wooden floor as he ran around the corner and out of sight.

'I know this is upsetting for you,' Josh began before she could speak, 'but we really must get a move on.'

She shook her head impatiently. 'Look, I've told you–'

Pressing a forefinger to her lips, he silenced her protest.

'Listen to me. Robbie had a fight with a playmate – but now it's over!' he reasoned practically, conscious of the minutes ticking by and the long drive ahead through rush-hour traffic. 'Once we're gone, he'll settle down. He'll soon be racing around as if it never happened.'

'But you heard him!' she exclaimed, her eyes wide and troubled. 'You saw how upset he was.'

'Kirsty, think what you're doing!' Josh demanded urgently. 'You've worked and waited for an opportunity like this. Don't let it slip away! You may never get another–'

'D'you think I don't know that?' she cried, her eyes sparkling up at him. 'But look – Kate Wakefield knows Robbie better than I do, yet it was me he asked for. It was me he ran to just now. I'm not going off and leaving him!'

'Fine. Then we'll take him with us,' Josh declared abruptly, his patience running low. Kirsty's heart tended to rule her head where her family was concerned. Somebody had to watch out for her interests. 'I can look after him while you're at the studios.'

'I'm not dragging him to Manchester and having him hanging around for hours while I audition!' Kirsty responded adamantly, flushing. 'He's a child! He doesn't even know you! What he needs is to go home. Now! With me … I'll have a word with

Kate.' She turned on her heel and made for the playroom. 'I'll see you in the car.'

They hardly spoke during the drive back to Chimneys.

'All those years of hard work,' Josh commented tersely, catching her eye in the mirror as she sat in the rear seat with Robbie. 'I can't believe you're just throwing it all away.'

'I'm not. There'll be other parts,' she replied positively, looking away so he couldn't read the doubt in her eyes. 'Anyhow, it's done now – and I don't want to talk about it.'

'Well, I do! I drove all night to–'

'I'm sorry you went to so much trouble for nothing!' she snapped. 'But I didn't ask you to come to Yorkshire.'

'That isn't what I meant and you know it!' he returned, stung by her sharpness. 'I came because I knew how important today was. Which is more than any of your family appears to do!'

'Josh!' She glared at him, casting a meaningful glance in Robbie's direction.

Josh inclined his head slightly. He was pale and Kirsty knew he was seething. But for Robbie's presence, they'd be quarrelling violently about the impulsive decision which had probably changed her life.

Once home, Robbie took his train and a pocketful of biscuits and happily dashed across the garden to the tree-house.

'At least he's happy now!' Kirsty sighed to herself, standing in the empty kitchen. It was less than an hour since she'd rushed from the house with such high hopes for her future. Now there was nothing.

'I'll telephone Manchester,' she remarked flatly, hearing Josh coming in through the back door. 'Tell them I'm not coming.'

'Do it in a minute.' He strode into the kitchen, tossing his car keys on to the table. 'First we have to talk – about you – about what's happening here.'

'Leave it, Josh. Please.' She shook her head wearily and leaned over to switch on the kettle. 'You're angry–'

'You bet I'm angry – but not with you!' he exploded impatiently. 'I'm angry *for* you. Your family is taking advantage of you. They're selfish and–'

She whirled around, her eyes flashing.

'You've no right to say that. You've never even met them!'

He didn't flinch from the indignation in her eyes.

'I love you. That gives me the right,' he said simply. 'D'you think I liked watching you choose between a child and your audition? You shouldn't have had to do it. Your mother ought to be here.'

'Mum can't be in two places at once!' Kirsty retaliated. 'Dorrie needs her in Auchlanrick.'

Josh sighed. 'Look, I'm sorry your sister's pregnant and unwell – but she's in hospital, getting the best possible care. And she has her husband. There's no reason for your mother to stay.'

'Graham can't be with Dorrie all the time,' Kirsty mumbled, her hands trembling as she set mugs on a tray. 'He has a business to run – and Mum reckons he's having problems.'

'What about *your* business?' Josh demanded furiously. 'Or don't your problems count? Now the crisis in Scotland is past, your mother could come back here. Instead, she's taking it for granted that you'll put your life on hold – even sacrifice your career.'

'I'm just helping out,' Kirsty muttered. 'It's just temporary.'

'Temporary has a habit of drifting into permanent,' he continued relentlessly. 'Nobody knows when Isobel and Douglas will be home. Suppose – they don't come home? Are you going to stay here for ever?'

Kirsty gasped at the horror of what he was suggesting, the tray almost falling from her unsteady hands. She set it down with a clatter, catching her lower lip between her teeth as he words echoed and re-echoed in her mind: 'Suppose they don't come home...'

'I'm sorry!' Josh pulled her into his arms, holding her tightly against him. 'I came to help you, not make you unhappy.'

'I – I wanted to stay with Robbie, but–' She broke off dejectedly, only too aware of everything she'd lost. 'I'm scared. I've already had to withdraw from that sportswear commercial and a few other jobs, too. I've been independent since I was eighteen. I'm used to making my own decisions. Suddenly things are happening and I'm not in control of my own life any more!'

'I wish I could do something,' he murmured.

'You're here,' she whispered simply.

Josh thought quickly.

'Look – it's ages since we've had a whole day together. Why don't we go up into the hills? Just the two – three – of us,' he amended with a grin, remembering Robbie. 'And this evening I'll take you out for a romantic dinner.'

'The hills'll be lovely,' she responded eagerly. Josh's smile always made her smile. 'But I can't go out tonight because–'

'–of the children!' he finished for her, and laughed, putting an arm about her shoulders. 'We'll stay in then.'

'Janey's meeting Marcus at the movies and Alasdair's never any trouble. Once Robbie's tucked up, we can have a quiet evening.' Kirsty's eyes were shining. 'I'll cook something nice. I'm getting pretty good, you know. What do you say?'

'Yes – on one condition,' he replied, gathering her to him again. 'I'll do the cooking!'

He was as good as his word, and while he was busy in the kitchen, Kirsty went up to check on Robbie.

Josh was lighting the candles on a table set for two when she returned.

'All that racing round today on the hills did the trick.' She grinned at him. 'He's sound asleep.'

'It was a good day–' He glanced up. 'You weren't wearing that a few minutes ago!'

She glanced down at the pretty blouse she

had slipped on, pleased that he had noticed.

'Special occasion,' she commented teasingly, and leaned across the table to kiss him. 'I felt like dressing up.'

'Careful!' He shielded the candle flame with his hand. 'Besides, dinner's ready.'

Josh's grandparents and mother were restaurateurs, and although he hadn't joined the business, Kirsty was convinced he could have become a top-class chef if he had wanted to.

'This is absolutely wonderful.' She sighed blissfully, chinking her glass to his. 'The food, the music, and especially–'

The back door banged open and slammed shut. Heels clicked rapidly along the hall.

'Must be Janey!' Kirsty remarked, startled, and she was on her feet and out of the sitting-room in a flash.

The teenager was at the foot of the stairs. One look at Kirsty's concerned face was enough – she burst into noisy tears, and didn't pull away when Kirsty put her arms about her.

'I waited and waited, but M-Marcus didn't come,' Janey gulped. 'And then – then–'

Josh had followed Kirsty, but he tactfully made himself scarce while Kirsty went with the distraught girl up to her bedroom.

'How is she?' he asked when Kirsty came down after a few minutes to make Janey some hot chocolate.

'Inconsolable,' she replied bleakly. 'Marcus was her first boyfriend. He not only stood her up tonight, but Janey saw him in town with another girl.'

'Poor kid..' Josh grimaced sympathetically, then paused. 'Look – I think I'll just slip away. I'd have to be going in an hour or so anyhow.'

Kirsty nodded. 'I'm sorry our evening was spoiled,' she said, gazing sadly at the cold remnants of their lovely dinner.

He gave a resigned shrug and kissed her goodbye. They'd said goodbye before. Faced long separations before. But somehow this felt different, and she clung to his arm as she accompanied him to his car.

'I'm sorry it's all gone wrong today,' she blurted out, leaning in through the car's open window to kiss him for the last time. 'But we'll sort something out. We'll find ways to be together. Won't we?'

He didn't answer before he switched on the engine and moved off.

She waved him out of sight, watching until the car's rear lights disappeared between the dark hedgerows before she returned indoors.

Taking the mugs of hot chocolate upstairs, Kirsty could hear Janey's sobbing and suddenly realised that her own eyes were wet.

She hesitated on the landing, unsure if the prickling tears were for her young niece – or for herself and Josh.

Chapter Seven

'The Babies Are Coming'

'Between you and me, Ena, I still lie awake worrying about her and the babies,' Ailsa was confiding to her friend as they walked back from the shops. 'But Dorrie's been so much brighter since the hospital discharged her. Being back in her own home has made a big difference.'

'Be sure to tell her I was asking after her,' Ena Hamilton said when they reached Ailsa's gate. 'And I'll bring round that pattern book this afternoon.'

'Thanks. We've made plenty of newborn things, but Dorrie's keen to get started on rompers and dresses.' Ailsa frowned slightly.

'Graham hasn't said as much, but he doesn't want Dorrie doing it. He doesn't like her making plans for after the twins are born, either. Myself, I think it's a good sign.' Ailsa took her key from her handbag. 'It's better for her to keep occupied and cheerful instead of fretting and fearing the worst.'

Ailsa had no sooner got indoors than she heard noises from the kitchen.

'Dorrie! What are you doing down here?' She shook her head anxiously. 'You should be in bed. You know what the doctors said.'

'Don't fuss, Mum,' Dorrie returned gently. 'I'm not an invalid, I just need to be careful. Graham's coming home for lunch and I want to make something special for him.'

'I'd have done it,' Ailsa protested. 'You only had to ask.'

'I know that, but you're already doing far too much.' Dorrie smiled ruefully. 'What with looking after Graham and the house, waiting on me hand and foot...'

Firmly Ailsa shepherded Dorrie from the kitchen.

'I'm happiest when I'm busy, you know that,' she assured her. 'I'll take over now. You go and put your feet up. You'll be rushed off them once those twins arrive,' she added.

'Come and talk to me, Mum,' Dorrie began soberly, going into the front room and sitting down. 'You know how you just mentioned the babies? Well, Graham never does any more. When I asked him about names – if he liked Tom and Lucy – he just nodded and changed the subject.' She shook her head in bewilderment. 'I love him more than ever, but sometimes I don't think I know him any better now than when we first married.' She raised disturbed eyes to Ailsa. 'I never know what he's really feeling – what's going on inside his head.'

'It's only his way,' Ailsa tried to reassure her. 'It doesn't mean anything's wrong. Graham's like your dad was. He's not the sort to show his feelings.'

When Ailsa returned to the kitchen, Dorrie was still restless to do something useful. Before her pregnancy had started to cause concern, she'd always handled the office side of Graham's painting and decorating business. And since coming home she'd often asked him to bring her the books so she could catch up on the paperwork. However, he had always refused.

Now, though, she opened the sideboard drawer and began to leaf through the bundles of letters, invoices and scraps of grimy paper. She'd soon sort this lot out!

She began to grow alarmed, however, when she found several unpaid bills and a letter of complaint from Chadwick's. She frowned. This wasn't like Graham! He was always so careful about paying bills promptly, and as for Chadwick's... Dorrie read their letter again with growing confusion.

Graham had been overjoyed when he'd won that contract to paint the canteen and redecorate the offices of their factory in town. Chadwick's was his first big customer, and he knew that if he did a good job for them it might lead to bigger and better things...

Yet now Chadwick's were complaining. Dorrie rubbed her fingertips against her forehead. None of it made any sense.

'Mum!' She hurried into the kitchen, the letter and bills still in her hands. 'Look at these! What do you think's going on?'

Ailsa glanced at the papers, and went to Dorrie's side, trying to usher her towards a chair.

'I'm sure it's nothing for you to get upset about.'

But Dorrie had seen a fleeting look in her mother's eyes, and knew that this wasn't the first time she had seen these papers, that this wasn't the shock to Ailsa that it was to herself.

'Stop it! You're doing exactly what Graham's been doing – shutting me out!' Dorrie's voice shook. 'I'm not a child. Tell me the truth. Is Graham in trouble?'

'Everything finished, Graham?' Stuart Donaldson called, pulling into the driveway of the newly refurbished cottage.

'Just about, Mr Donaldson.' Graham hadn't stopped loading the cans of paint into his van when the sporty saloon had drawn up alongside. 'It's all ready for you to move in.'

'I'll just take a look!' Donaldson grinned, disappearing through the low front door.

Graham glanced after him, his eyes lingering on the attractive, cream-washed stone cottage.

He and his elder brother, Jim, had been born in a similar cottage. But theirs had been a working croft, with few comforts. Graham had seen his parents – both dead now – struggling to scratch a meagre living and sworn he'd never live like that. He'd fought bitterly with Jim because of it...

'You've done a good job, Graham.' Stuart Donaldson emerged cheerfully, pushing his hands into the pockets of his jeans. 'It looks splendid. My fiancée's going to be delighted.'

'Ay, it's a fine wee house,' Graham answered stiffly, unable to suppress a surge of resentment.

If only he could have bought Dorrie somewhere like this when they were first married. But they'd still been in their teens, and if Ailsa hadn't offered to share her house, they wouldn't have been able to get married at all.

Besides, Dorrie had wanted to live with her mother. She'd been upset at the idea of leaving Ailsa on her own.

Graham was fond of Ailsa, but he had never felt comfortable living under her roof. He didn't like being beholden to anyone, and when he'd started up his own business he'd been determined that, one day, Dorrie and he would have a house of their own.

And where had all his fancy ambitions got him? Graham sighed. Instead of prospering, he was getting sucked deeper and deeper into problems he couldn't see any way out of.

'Zoe won't be here until later – wedding dress fitting!' Stuart Donaldson was saying, still admiring the cottage. 'Would you like to join me in the pub for some lunch, Graham?'

'No, thanks, Mr Donaldson. I'm looking in at home to check that my wife's OK, then I've to get straight into town,' he replied. 'I'm due at Chadwick's this afternoon.'

When he got home, Graham was nearly as surprised as Ailsa had been to find Dorrie up and about. But when he made comment, Dorrie protested, 'Don't you start. You sound just like Mum! I feel fine, really I do. And since this is the first lunch-time you've been able to get home for ages, I've made your favourite pasties.'

'You made them?' he queried with concern. Although he'd noticed she was looking better, there was no sense in taking unnecessary chances. 'You shouldn't go overdoing things.'

'I haven't!' she exclaimed in good-natured exasperation. 'Mum did most of the real work.'

'Where is Ailsa?' he asked, washing his hands at the kitchen sink.

'WI.' She bent carefully to take the pasties out of the oven.

'I'll do that!' Graham insisted hurriedly, taking the hot baking tray. 'They look great, but I haven't much time. I have to be on my way to Chadwick's by half-past.'

She'd intended to leave it until evening,

when they'd have time to talk, but it seemed like fate that the subject had come up now.

She drew a deep breath and plunged in.

'Graham – about Chadwick's... I was looking through the books this morning and I saw all those unpaid bills. And the letter from Chadwick's... Why didn't you tell me things were so bad?'

'Oh, it's not that bad!' he replied confidently. 'It's just that some of my customers are late in paying, so I'm short of cash to pay my own bills. As for Chadwick's – well, I may have bitten off a bit more than I can chew, but it's nothing a few extra hours of solid graft won't put right.'

'You're hardly ever home as it is,' she murmured anxiously. In truth he looked worn out.

He shrugged carelessly. 'I'm not afraid of hard work. Especially now I've something to work for. You, and–' He hesitated, gazing down at her. '–and our family.'

'Tom and Lucy,' she whispered, touching his cheek. 'Don't worry, darling. Everything's going to be all right this time. I can't explain how I know – but I do!'

He nodded wordlessly. She sounded so certain, he feared for her anew. How would she cope if something did go wrong?

'I've been indoors so long, I'd love to go out in the sunshine and walk and walk and walk!' She smiled up at him. 'Up to the loch and have a picnic like we did when we were courting!'

'That's out of the question.' He returned her smile. 'Suppose we settle for having lunch in the back garden?'

He was fetching the folding chairs from the shed when he heard a clatter in the kitchen and looked through the open window.

'Dorrie?'

'It's all right. Just knocked over the tea caddy!'

'Give me a shout when it's ready and I'll come and carry it.'

'Thanks, I'll be glad when – Graham!' She caught a sharp breath, but her voice stayed perfectly calm. 'Graham – I think you'd better come...'

Tom and Lucy were born early that evening. For a very few, precious moments, Dorrie and Graham were allowed to hold their babies before they were taken to the Special Care Unit.

'I can hardly believe it. They're so perfect,' Dorrie murmured contentedly as Graham helped her snuggle down into bed in the quiet, private room. 'And so tiny!'

Even Tom, the bigger and heavier twin, had fitted easily upon his palm, and Graham's large, rough hands had felt so huge and clumsy he'd been scared of touching the curling little fingers and toes.

'The clothes we've knitted will be far too big,' Dorrie remarked drowsily, leaning her head against Graham as he sat beside her on the bed. 'But you can get especially small things for premature babies. Will you ask Mum about it?'

'Oh, there'll be time enough for that tomorrow. You get some rest now,' he said, patting her hand. 'The doctor said I was to pop along to the unit for a minute or two. Will you be all right on your own?'

'Mmm.' She sighed sleepily, turning her head on the pillow. 'Will you put their picture where I can see it?'

He propped the instant photograph of the babies on the bedside cabinet and left the room.

The moment the door closed behind him, Dorrie felt horribly alone. Wide awake and gripped by cold, overwhelming fear, she reached out and picked up the photograph. A dry sob escaped her throat as she gazed helplessly at the two crumpled little faces.

She wanted her babies. Wanted to hold them – have them with her. But all she had was their photograph, and the desperate hope that Tom and Lucy would be strong enough to survive their first, critical hours of life.

'Dr Blundell...?' The soldier – they could see he was a sergeant now – spoke in a questioning tone. 'Please – step forward.'

As Douglas did as he was ordered, the light was tilted to shine full in his face. Instinctively he raised an arm to shield his eyes, and a dozen more soldiers emerged from the night. Their automatic weapons were menacingly levelled on the group of four trapped in their circle.

'My men react quickly. I advise you not to do anything else which might be misunderstood.'

The sergeant waved his hand, and the soldiers melted like shadows into the darkness. It was as he half turned to focus his complete attention on his prisoners once more that Douglas caught a clear glimpse of him.

'Soler!'

'You never expected to see me again!' the sergeant remarked with a humourless laugh, then indicated the large bark-thatched sorting shed which had doubled as Douglas's office. 'Wait for me in there. Just Blundell!' he added sharply as the others moved to follow.

Isobel continued to cling to Douglas's arm and after a brief, intense stare, the sergeant nodded his permission for her to go with him.

'How does he know you, Douglas?' she demanded when they were alone in the relative safety of the shed. 'Who is he?'

'His name's Enrique Soler,' Douglas explained, surveying the shed with its rows of floor-to-ceiling stacking shelves. The results of almost a full year's excavation had been stored in here.

Thankfully little appeared to have been damaged or even disturbed. Nothing of obvious value to interest looters, he supposed.

He automatically righted his overturned desk, picked up his chair and a bench and gathered up some scattered documents. His coal-oil lamp had fallen upon the plankboard floor, but amazingly the smoke-stained glass chimney wasn't even cracked.

'The Soler brothers were employed by the dig,' he went on matter-of-factly, taking a book of matches from his desk drawer and lighting the lamp. 'Enrique was my fore-man.'

'Then he won't harm us, will he?' she pressed, Douglas's methodical calmness heightening her agitation. 'Not if he's your friend!'

'Do you remember the day after you arrived in Castildoro?' he asked quietly. 'When Angie and Karl told us camping equipment had been stolen from the site and several workers hadn't turned up? Enrique and his brothers were amongst them.'

'I remember.' She stared up at him. 'You said he was a decent man and you trusted him.'

'I know I did – but this country is at war with itself. Even the closest friends will find themselves on opposite sides. I liked and respected Enrique, but I was his employer, nothing more. He's turned his back on everything – his family, his home – and become a thief to volunteer for Ortega's army.' He met her eyes despairingly. 'He's a soldier now. There's no point in hoping–'

Douglas broke off as the shed door swung open and Soler strode inside, the heels of his boots jarring on the hollow plankboard. Past him, through the open door, the site appeared to be deserted.

'Where are Angie and Karl?' Douglas demanded. 'What have you done with them?'

Soler didn't answer. He sauntered between the couple and seated himself casually at Douglas's desk.

'Our situations are reversed now,' he remarked with a wry smile. 'You may not be aware that the capital city has fallen. Castildoro is ours, Dr Blundell. Soon the whole country will be ours.'

'What about my colleagues?' Douglas persisted, his fingers clenching around Isobel's hand. 'Where are Angie and Karl?'

Again Soler chose not to answer the question.

'Nobody will get hurt provided you co-operate,' he stated smoothly. 'Where are the others?'

Douglas feigned a look of bewilderment.

'Others? There are no others,' he answered warily. 'Just us four.'

'Lying is pointless. We have found the wreckage of the plane. We know who was aboard!' Soler's palm slammed flat on to the desk. 'Those three men are enemies of the state. I ask you the question again: where are they? Where is Luis Rosales?'

If Isobel had ever heard the name before,

she was too frightened to remember. Douglas, however, realised the truth immediately – the former president's only son had been with them on Sam Fraser's plane. And it made their situation even more dangerous. General Ortega would stop at nothing to capture him...

'We don't know where the others are!' Isobel cried out impulsively. 'We split up after the plane crashed. We don't know where they are!'

The fact that she was speaking the truth gave her words a conviction she could not have faked and Soler seemed to sense this.

He looked from her to Douglas, his eyes narrowing thoughtfully.

'It is my duty to take you back to Castildoro for further interrogation,' he commented finally. 'However, I am deeply in your debt, Dr Blundell. After my brothers and I stole from you, you had the power to make our family pay for what we had done. But you did not.'

He rose, formally extending his hand.

'Consequently I have an obligation to help you. But I do not want to know where you are going – or when you are leaving.'

'We need rest,' Douglas replied cautiously, accepting Soler's gesture of conciliation.

'And enough time to collect supplies and repair the station-wagon.'

'I will report that the site has been searched. You should be safe here for a time,' Soler remarked, starting for the door. 'But if another unit does discover you, I can do nothing.'

'What about your men?' Isobel ventured hesitantly. 'They know we're here.'

Soler turned to look at her.

'My men do what I tell them, Mrs Blundell. They will say nothing. However, it might be prudent to construct a hiding place in case of emergency.' He paused at the door to tap the hollow sounding plankboards with the sole of his boot. 'I supervised the laying of the foundations for this shed. A crawl-space could soon be dug out beneath the flooring.

'When I am off duty, Dr Blundell,' Soler concluded in a low voice, before stepping out into the moonlight, 'I will come again.'

Digging the hiding place became their priority. After only a few hours' sleep, Douglas and Karl – who had been held, unharmed, outside the office with Angie during Douglas and Isobel's interview with Soler – started work later that night.

Levering up a section of the plank-boarding, they enlarged the gap between floor and ground. Then they hammered in new beams for extra support and to lessen the echoing hollowness which might arouse the suspicions of somebody walking over the hiding place.

During the days that followed, they were meticulous about tidiness. Accidentally leaving something lying about might signal their presence if a military patrol passed by. They also avoided lighting fires for cooking, and pushed Angela's station-wagon out of sight so they could repair it.

'Lunch, Karl. Tomato soup – straight from the can!' Angela announced one day, entering the radio hut where he spent every spare moment.

Karl had been a radio enthusiast since boyhood, and although the equipment had been damaged, he was convinced that he would be able to coax it into working order.

'How's it going?' she asked, looking curiously at the bewildering array of dials and sensors.

Karl was pleased with his efforts and gave an optimistic smile.

'Pretty promising! I picked up a radio ham and kept repeating a message. I'm not sure he heard me, but it's a start.'

'Well done!' She turned and set the soup bowl and a mug of coffee on the table beside him.

'Thanks.' He smiled up at her, lightly covering her hand with his, but at that moment Angela dropped the plastic soup spoons and had to withdraw her hand to retrieve them. It appeared perfectly natural, but it wasn't – and Karl knew it.

'Angela – can't we try?' he murmured.

'What good would it do?' she asked. 'We've already discussed this, Karl.'

'But we were virtual strangers then,' he persisted. 'Everything's different now.'

Angie shook her head. 'All that's changed is that instead of being in New York, we're out in the middle of nowhere. Look, Karl – we're colleagues and friends – can't you be content with that?'

At a sound outside she pushed aside the green canvas blind and glanced from the glassless window to see an ageing pick-up truck chugging and bouncing towards them along the rough track.

'Here's Soler,' she told him. 'Are you coming out?'

Karl shook his head, turning back to the radio.

'I've nearly got this thing fixed. Better I

stick at it.'

Isobel and Douglas were helping Enrique Soler unload a variety of cardboard boxes when Angela joined them. He'd brought medical supplies, provisions, bottled water, a bundle of shapeless shirts, shorts and hats similar to those he himself was wearing and, most importantly, a replacement tyre.

'I noticed the station-wagon had a puncture,' he commented, reaching into the truck. 'And here's gasoline. Use it cautiously – it's in short supply right now.'

'This is tremendous, Enrique!' Douglas responded gratefully. 'I can't–'

He was interrupted by a high-pitched shriek from the radio hut and Karl's yell of triumph.

Even before the others had time to realise what was happening, Enrique Soler had snatched up the jack from his truck and was racing across the site.

He burst into the cramped hut with a shout of anger.

'I told you not to use the radio!'

Slowly, deliberately, Karl got to his feet to confront the younger man.

'I don't take orders from you, Soler! A radio link with the outside world is our best chance–'

'*Your* best chance?' Soler interrupted savagely. 'I've put my life – and the lives of my family – at risk by helping you. Don't you realise what you've done?' he cried.

Soler slammed the jack down on the radio in a single blow, smashing the equipment irreparably. Then without another word, he strode from the hut and started up his truck. In a cloud of dust he swerved from the site and on to the rough track toward Castildoro.

Shocked and unnerved by the violence of his reaction, Douglas and Karl decided they'd better leave at once instead of in another day or two as planned.

Haste made them less careful than usual and it was purely by chance that Angela heard the vehicles as she was filling her station-wagon with petrol.

Edging through the bushes to see the track, what she saw made her eyes open wide.

Tossing the can aside, she raced back to the site where the others were packing up.

'It's Soler! He's back!' she warned breathlessly, her lungs bursting. 'In uniform. Not alone. Must be twenty or thirty–'

Grabbing both women by the arms, Douglas propelled them toward the sorting shed. There was nothing they could do about their belongings that lay strewn everywhere.

Inside, Karl raised the false section of plankboard. First Isobel and Angela, then Karl, and finally Douglas himself, squeezed into the crawl-space.

Crouching there in the blackness, they scarcely dared to breathe.

They could see nothing. Only hear.

Engines. Footsteps. Voices…

Enrique Soler's voice spoke respectfully as he led his commanding officer directly towards their hiding place…

The two men paused outside the shed, their voices carrying clearly through the glassless window.

As the officer fired questions, Soler answered hesitantly but with obvious respect.

Isobel couldn't understand what was being said but she managed to pick out the name Luis Rosales several times. She was terrified, lying there in the darkness, not knowing if Enrique Soler was betraying them.

'Karl's radio signals were picked up,' Angela murmured, her mouth pressed close to Isobel's ear. 'I think Soler's in trouble for not finding us before.'

She strained to listen through the racket of a further hurried, violent search.

'But he hasn't turned us in – yet!' she added.

The claustrophobic blackness of their cramped hiding space was overwhelming. Isobel bit her lip to stop herself gasping aloud as Soler and his captain stood directly overhead, their boots sending grit showering through the floorboards.

They spoke rapidly. Isobel and the others lay still. Waiting. Listening. Praying.

'Soler's to take all the dig's records,' Angela breathed.

Minutes seemed like hours until, at last, the captain strode out of the shed. Engines started up. Apparently the search party was withdrawing.

However, Enrique Soler still lingered above them.

'If ever we meet again, Dr Blundell–' his low voice was no longer friendly '–it will be as enemies.' Then he, too, was gone.

Chapter Eight

Poor Robbie...

They remained hidden until evening. Then, clinging to the shadows, they fled to the forest clearing where Angela's station-wagon was hidden.

With Angela driving as fast as she dared, and everybody talking loudly and at once, Isobel's thoughts unexpectedly returned to Soler. He had already taken so many chances for them, and risked so much personal danger. They were for ever in his debt. But what would happen to him if the military ever discovered he had helped them to escape?

Sam Fraser had given Douglas instructions about the route he, Luis and Cesar Bernaldez intended to take to the border. Progress was steady, and surprisingly quickly Angela was skirting a little-used railroad track.

A solitary figure emerged from the bushes. It was Sam.

After they had greeted each other, Angela

found herself gazing beyond him to where Cesar Bernaldez was slumped in the shade of a tree. He was alone.

She looked enquiringly at Sam. 'Where's Luis?'

'Gone for food.' Sam jerked a thumb. 'We take it in turns.'

She pocketed her keys and strode away from the car.

'Angela!' he called warningly.

'I'll be careful!'

She met Luis returning from a share-cropper's home, a rucksack of provisions slung across his shoulder.

His eyes lit up when he saw her.

'Angela! You're safe! I was sure—' He broke off awkwardly, then moved forward to enfold her in a tentative embrace. 'Thank God you're all right!'

'We very nearly weren't!' she observed wryly. 'I'll explain later. What about you?' She searched his unshaven face. Luis looked so much older: unkempt, shabby… Just another itinerant labourer seeking work… 'Are you OK?'

'Yes. But do you know anything about my father?' he demanded. 'The only newspapers we've seen are days old and filled with Ortega's propaganda. Do you know what's happened to him? Have they captured him?'

'No – he's safe,' she answered simply. 'We never actually reached Castildoro, but I was told your father and his government left before Ortega took the city. They went into exile.'

Luis bowed his head for a moment.

'It's civil war. There are still some men loyal to my father who are opposing Ortega. They're defending democracy... My country is fighting for its very life!' He looked away from her as they walked, frustrated and deeply ashamed. 'Yet I do nothing to help. I hide behind an old man – pretend to be someone I'm not!'

'Getting killed wouldn't be much use either,' Angela responded briskly. 'Your chance will come, Luis – and when it does you'll be as brave as anyone!'

'I wonder about that,' he answered frankly. 'I watch the planes, hear the gunfire, and I wonder...'

They continued in silence until the rusted rails came into view.

'Did you see Cesar?' Luis asked suddenly, glancing at her. 'How do you think he looks?'

'Tired,' she replied guardedly. She didn't want Luis to guess how shocked she'd been at the deterioration in the old man's condition. 'But travelling will be much easier for him with the car.'

'It's too late.' Angela saw that Luis was crying, making no attempt to conceal the tears spilling from his dark eyes. 'Cesar is dying,' he announced bluntly.

She didn't say anything. What *could* she say? She knew as well as he did that the old man was very sick indeed. It was pointless to deny it.

Following the railroad line drew them deeper into remote country. Whole days slipped past without them seeing a single other person.

Although running out of fuel was a constant worry in itself, the fear was all the more acute since everyone was all too keenly aware that Cesar Bernaldez was no longer capable of proceeding on foot.

'Noguera grew up around the mine,' Sam told them when the town lay just a short distance ahead. 'When the mine played out, Noguera pretty much closed down with it. But trains still pass through.'

Spreading the map across the bonnet of the car, he traced the track.

'It stops at all these little towns and villages in the mountains. It goes within a mile of the border at Gaviria. That's where we'll get off and cross.'

'Sounds easy enough,' Douglas remarked dryly.

'No, but–' Sam began, then noticed Isobel's apprehensive expression. 'Don't worry, there's no checkpoint. There's not even a marker to show where this country ends and the next begins. Once we board the train, you're practically on your way home!'

Clean-shaven and wearing a newly acquired second-hand shirt and blue jeans, Luis was selected to go into Noguera to find out when the next train was due. He was pulling on his rucksack when Angela decided she would go with him.

However, as she hurried to collect her own rucksack, Isobel followed her.

'Do you think this is wise?' she inquired with some concern.

Angela shrugged. 'What could be more innocent than a couple of students trying to get away from the fighting?'

'That isn't what I meant,' Isobel pressed on uncomfortably. 'I don't want to interfere, but ... well, perhaps you're not aware of it, but Karl is quite concerned that you're spending too much time with Luis.'

Angela sighed and turned to look at the older woman.

'Karl's just jealous,' she retorted bluntly, then went on to explain: 'When I arrived in New York, Karl had just been divorced. We were both lonely and we went out a few times. That's all there was between us – and that's all there ever will be.'

Hitching the rucksack into position and settling it on her shoulders, she went on, 'But you're right about one thing, Isobel – it isn't any of your business!'

Angela and Luis were sweltering and dust streaked when they reached Noguera shortly after noon. To their relief, the town showed no signs of military presence.

When they got to the station, however, the ticket window was boarded up. An elderly man, seated at the far end of the paint-peeled platform, was watching them curiously and after a quick glance around Luis approached him.

The man nodded amiably in response to his inquiry.

'Three, maybe four, trains come through a month. Stop for water and coal. But you have just missed one. Now there will not be another till next week. Of course, if you really want a train–' His features creased into a broken-toothed grin '–there is one sitting waiting for you out there.' He pointed vaguely off to the west. 'Just get up a head of steam and off you go!'

Luis wasn't sure if the old man was joking. 'What do you mean?' he asked.

The old man's expression became grave.

'It was carrying resistance fighters. Ortega attacked it. They just left the train standing out there on the spur. It is yours for the taking.'

When Luis and Angela rejoined the others he recounted what the old man had told them.

'Sounds fantastic – but I suppose we might as well take a look,' was Sam's assessment, and they set off along the track.

They found the ancient locomotive exactly as the old man had described it – bullet-scarred and abandoned, a few miles west of Noguera.

'Too slow to be useful to Ortega's troops,' Sam Fraser commented with satisfaction, jumping down from the engine after a cursory inspection. 'But she's still got plenty of coal and water. Provided you two are willing to get your hands dirty–' he glanced at Douglas and Karl '–we'll be on our way by morning.'

Despite Sam's confident prediction, it was

another twenty-four hours before the train was ready to move by which time knots of people had gathered around it, sitting on the ground in orderly groups with bundles of weaving, boxes of produce, sacks of cacao and strings of tobacco.

'Let them on,' Sam decreed, brusquely sweeping aside Douglas and Karl's protests. 'There'll be a commotion if we don't. In fact, it's not a bad idea to take on passengers all along the line. A trainful of folk going to market will be a lot less conspicuous than a train carrying just half a dozen Europeans.'

They had to concede the logic of his argument so directed the huddles of people aboard.

The rattling carriages were crammed to bursting by the time the mountains of Gaviria slid into sight almost a week later. Sam had been driving since dawn, and Isobel manoeuvred through the crowded, lurching train with a flask of fresh coffee.

'Thanks.' He flexed the stiffness from his neck and shoulder muscles, and gestured to the flask. 'Will you keep me company? It gets pretty lonely up here!'

She smiled. 'All right.'

'How's Cesar?' Sam asked after a minute.

'Resting in the guard's van. We've made him as comfortable as possible,' she answered sadly. 'At least Luis is with him.'

He nodded. Isobel didn't need to say more.

She stood next to him, sipping the hot, bitter coffee, gazing out of the window but not looking at anything in particular. The railroad was winding between the mountains, the sides of the ravine narrow and rising steeply with patches of florid poppies, clumps of spearthorn and trees that reminded her of stunted Scots pines.

'Legend has it that a mighty god lives inside these mountains. The ravine's echo is his voice,' Sam commented.

He'd taken his eye from the track only briefly, but as he turned back he began dragging on the brake as the train rattled around a curve.

The locked wheels screeched, spitting sparks.

Sam's gaze was riveted on the fallen tree sprawled across the line.

Isobel was staring, too, yet somehow never doubting that he would stop the train in time.

She didn't know what made her glance upwards at that precise moment, but what she saw terrified her. Motionless against the cornflower blue sky was a ragged line of troops. And even as she stared at them they began to move.

She gasped Sam's name as, firing warning shots, the soldiers came pouring down into the ravine.

'I passed Janey in the lane,' Winifred remarked, letting herself into the house. 'Still moping, is she?'

'She really cared for Marcus,' Kirsty sighed. 'Losing him will hurt more than any physical pain.'

'That sounds like the voice of experience,' Winifred commented, hanging up her cardigan. 'Or am I being too nosey?'

Kirsty smiled forlornly. 'No. You're right on, as usual!'

She led the other woman into the kitchen.

'Fancy a coffee and a piece of chocolate cake? I've just finished the icing. Kate Wakefield's popping in for a chat about eleven and she's such a capable person I felt I had to bake something fancy! Paul Ashworth's coming, too,' she went on. 'He's Robbie's godfather – and very good with him.'

Winifred surveyed the rich chocolate cake with its hazelnut paste filling and glistening coffee frosting.

'Looks lovely, I must say – but I shouldn't,' she protested half-heartedly.

Kirsty shrugged. 'I shouldn't either – but I will if you will!'

'Oh, go on then!'

Kirsty cut two extremely generous slices and poured out the coffee, and once they were sitting opposite each other at the kitchen table, she looked across at the motherly older woman.

'Missing that audition seems to have changed things between Josh and me,' she told her.

'You've not seen each other since, have you?' Winifred stirred her coffee absent-mindedly. 'Letters and phone calls are all right, but it's easy to get the wrong end of the stick when you're not face to face.'

'It's more than that. We're drifting apart, I can feel it,' Kirsty confided unhappily. 'He's working at the recording company's studios near Paris. It was arranged ages ago and he's rented a flat. I could have gone with him… My part in his life is getting smaller and smaller.' She paused, gazing unseeingly at the willow-patterned dishes on the dresser. 'How long can I expect him to wait?'

'It hasn't been that long…' Winifred

reasoned. 'Even if it seems like it.'

'It's not that I don't trust him. I do!' Kirsty went on, absorbed in her tangled thoughts. 'But I just can't help – worrying. We're hundreds of miles apart and Josh is alone. What if he finds someone else?'

All Winifred could do was be as sympathetic and reassuring as she knew how.

Kate and Paul arrived separately but at the same time a few minutes later, and Kirsty showed them into the sitting-room, leaving them to chat while she fetched the coffee and cake.

'Since that little spat he had, Robbie hasn't wanted to go to playschool,' Kirsty explained when the three were settled. 'He gets upset whenever I mention it, so I haven't pushed him. He starts proper school in September, you see, and I don't want to risk putting him off.'

Kate nodded sympathetically. 'I appreciate your concern, but I honestly don't think keeping him at home is the answer,' she returned, and glanced briefly to Paul for support, but his attention was focused on Kirsty. 'Playschool is a rehearsal for the children,' she went on. 'Learning to cope with ups and downs and different and challenging situations is valuable experience for when they start school.'

'Robbie won't always be able to stay at home when he has a problem,' Paul observed. 'And I'm sure Kate will make certain there's no more bullying,' he added, glancing at the other woman.

'You can rest assured about that!' Kate agreed immediately.

Kirsty hesitated, wondering what was best for Robbie. If only Isobel was here – but there was no point in thinking about that. She would have to work it out for herself.

'I expect you're both right,' she eventually replied with a slight frown. 'I'll bring him in tomorrow.'

Next morning was gloriously summery, and the instant she got up, Kirsty went around the house flinging wide the windows and doors. Janey and Robbie were still asleep, but Alasdair must have crept from the house at the crack of dawn to go bird watching.

Kirsty was well into her daily exercise routine in the garden when she spotted him coming back along the beck. He waved and went indoors – then came racing out again.

'Auntie Kirsty! Robbie's not in bed!' he shouted. 'His duffel-bag and panda are gone. I – I think he's run away!'

'Oh, no!' Helplessly she scanned the rambling garden, the fast-flowing river and the woods beyond. So many places where a little boy could be in danger!

'You look around out here,' she urged Alasdair. 'I'll check the house.'

Alasdair nodded, shouting 'I'll yell if I find him!' as he raced across the grass.

Having started in the attics and worked downwards, Kirsty was in the hall when Winifred Bell arrived, and together they searched the large, cluttered cellars where there were so many places for a small child to hide.

'No,' Winifred finally muttered breathlessly, hands on hips. 'He's not here.'

'What if–' Kirsty began, but broke off when she heard heavy footfalls along the hall.

'Kirsty! Alasdair's just told me!' Paul shouted down through the cellar doorway. 'How on earth did Robbie manage to disappear from the house at this hour?'

'I was in the garden,' she answered distractedly, hurrying to join him, her imagination churning. Where could Robbie be? Suppose he'd tried to cross the beck? Or wandered off on to the moors? If anything happened to him... 'He – he must've slipped past me...'

'And you didn't even notice?' Paul retorted

sharply, catching her arm. 'How could you be so irresponsible?'

'Thank you, Paul, but I don't need you blaming me. I'm already blaming myself enough for both of us!' she cut in, her eyes bright. 'If you can't do anything more useful than– Listen, that's Alasdair!'

Kirsty was off and running from the house even as Paul heard the second shout.

'Robbie's under the bridge!' Alasdair pointed to the sturdy little stone affair that crossed the beck at the foot of the garden. 'He won't come out!'

'I'll see to him. Thanks, Alasdair! You were great.' She laughed with sheer relief. 'Go and have your breakfast. You've earned it.'

Scrambling on hands and knees down the muddy bank, she peered under the arching, lichened stones. Robbie's big eyes stared back at her.

'So you're running away, eh?' she asked calmly, squeezing in to sit cross-legged beside him. 'I wish you'd told me. We got a big fright when you weren't in bed.'

He sniffed loudly, but didn't say anything.

'Is it playschool?' she prompted after a minute, not looking at him. 'In case you get teased again about your glasses?'

'Jason'll hit me if I go back,' Robbie

177

mumbled finally, fidgeting with his duffel-bag.

'Kate wouldn't let him hurt you again,' she reassured. 'You know she wouldn't.'

Robbie shook his head doubtfully. 'He'll punch me when she's not looking. That's what he did before.'

'Suppose you stay at home a bit longer then?' she suggested. 'You and I can draw and read exactly as you would at playschool and then when you're ready to go back, you won't have missed anything. Would you like that, Robbie?'

Slowly the child nodded.

'Great!' She eased the duffel-bag from his clenched fists and wriggled from beneath the bridge, reaching back for Robbie's hand. 'Out you come then. I'll give you a start of five, then race you to breakfast!'

With all his problems solved, the little boy happily dashed for the house. Kirsty didn't follow, though, for Paul was standing glaring at her, having overheard the exchange.

'You should have been firmer,' he reproved. 'This could have ended in disaster.'

Kirsty felt irritation rising in her.

'You think I don't realise that?' she ground out. 'He's four years old, Paul! He's missing his mum and dad … and being teased and bullied at playschool. Running off was a cry for help. People don't always use words to ask for what they need, you know – especially when they're only four years old!'

Paul wasn't to be persuaded.

'You overreacted, giving into him like that. Why must you be so emotional?' he went on in a weary tone. 'You're always rushing headlong into situations without a thought for the consequences. The three of us agreed on the wisest way to tackle Robbie's difficulties. Now he'll assume–'

'All right, all right!' Kirsty exploded. 'So I'm not an expert like Kate. So I don't know the children as well as you do. But they're in my care, Paul – and I'm doing what I'd do if they were my own children, and if you – or Kate – have a problem with that,' Kirsty finished, starting swiftly up the path away from him, 'well, it's just too bad!'

That afternoon, she was at one end of the kitchen table scribbling a letter while Winifred sat at the other, polishing some brasses.

'Want me to post that?' the older woman offered, nodding to indicate the letter.

'No, thanks.' Kirsty gave her a rueful smile. 'To tell you the truth, I don't actually want to send it,' she confessed. 'It's to Gwen, my flatmate,' she continued, leaning back in her chair. 'I'm giving up my room. I can't afford to go on paying my share of the rent.'

Winifred paused in her polishing, looking thoughtful.

'I hadn't really thought about that,' she remarked, 'but it must be hard for you, not working.'

Kirsty shrugged, folding the notepaper into its envelope. 'I've hung on to the flat as long as I can. But as Paul pointed out, it's a waste of money keeping a place in London now I'm living here.'

Winifred rubbed a horse-brass hard.

'Once he told us about that radio message saying Isobel and Douglas were safe, I thought they'd be home in no time,' she commented.

Kirsty nodded. 'I did, too. But, like Paul and Alasdair keep telling us, it is a big country,' she reflected, 'and a troubled one. All the civilian airports and telephone links are closed. Paul reckons it could be months before Izzie and Douglas can get out. He's keeping up pressure on the Foreign Office to find–'

An impatient rapping at the front door interrupted her, and Winifred rose.

'I'll get it,' she offered. 'It's probably the

Scouts for the old papers.'

She returned after a minute or two laden with flowers.

'It wasn't the Scouts!' she commented unnecessarily and chuckled, setting the lavishly arranged floral basket down on the table in front of Kirsty, who was speechless. 'Well, don't just sit there gawping,'Winifred chided her. 'Open the card! What does he say?'

Carefully Kirsty extracted the card and scanned it.

'They're from Josh,' she whispered, her eyes soft. 'He's got a few days off and he's coming up so we can be together.'

'There now!' Winifred smiled broadly, as pleased as Punch. 'Things'll work out now, you'll see.'

'I hope so!' Kirsty murmured, and squeezed the older woman's shoulders in gratitude for her understanding. 'Is that the time? I'd better go and get changed!'

In less than ten minutes she was downstairs again, wearing a swimsuit and carrying a bundle of fluffy towels, but as she stepped into the kitchen she pulled up short.

'Hello, Kirsty.'

'Paul!' she greeted him warily.

'Seeing as how you two were fighting like cat and dog this morning,' Winifred commented, gathering up her cloths, 'I'll just go and polish the door-knocker!' and she tactfully withdrew.

'I want to apologise,' Paul began as soon as they were alone. 'For blaming–'

'I bit your head off, too,' Kirsty interrupted mildly, smiling. 'But we were both anxious about Robbie. Let's just forget it.'

'No. I shouldn't have criticised you like that,' he persisted. 'You're doing a fine job with the children.'

'I couldn't manage without Winifred's help – or yours. You've been wonderful,' she responded impulsively. 'Not just with the children, but with all – all the official stuff,' she faltered, suddenly conscious that he was studying her intently. 'I – er – promised the boys a swim in the beck before tea. I can find a pair of Douglas's trunks for you, if you'd like to join us.'

'No time,' he replied regretfully. 'I'm on my way to a meeting in Leeds. But I'll collect you tomorrow, about one, for Janey's sports' day?'

'OK.' She was still aware of his intense gaze and it was making her uncomfortable. 'See you then.'

'Yes.'

He continued to watch her as she walked

down the garden to the river, a lean, vibrant figure. He didn't even look round when Winifred came into the kitchen behind him.

'Living here has changed her. Settled her,' he commented.

'Maybe, but her heart's still in London,' Winifred returned bluntly.

'That Josh character?' he queried disparagingly. 'It's not serious. How can it be? She's only known him five minutes.'

'And I've known you since you were in short trousers. I don't want to see you get hurt again.' Winifred's brow knitted. 'Take my advice, lad, and forget any ideas of getting her back.'

Paul sighed. 'I can't. She's the only woman I've ever asked to marry me.' He glanced around from the window. 'I still love her.'

Chapter Nine

'It's The End…'

'All set?' Graham inquired with a cautious smile, looking around the door of the hospital room.

Dorrie looked up from the open suitcase and glanced around her. All her belongings had been packed. The twins' pictures were safely in her handbag.

She gave a helpless shrug.

'I don't want to go home. What if they need me and I'm not here?'

Without answering Graham snapped the suitcase shut and swung it from the bed, then, taking her arm, lead her out into the corridor. He never knew what to say when Dorrie talked like this.

'I want to see them just once more,' she murmured, holding back as they made for the lift. 'To say goodbye.'

'You've already said it a dozen times. The last time they were fast asleep,' Graham reasoned, not releasing his hold on her arm.

He knew that leaving Tom and Lucy behind in the hospital must be awful for Dorrie, but it had to be done.

'Come on.' He pressed the lift's call button. 'It's best.'

She seemed about to comply, then froze.

'Do you hear that?' she exclaimed, her eyes wide. 'It's Tom!'

'It can't be–'

Shaking free of Graham's grasp, she hurried from the lift and back along the corridor to the Special Care Unit.

Graham went after her, and his heart sank when he saw her standing with her palms pressed flat against the large plate glass windows of the unit. She was trembling as she gazed down at her babies.

'See? Both still asleep.' Graham pulled her gently away. 'Come on, love, it's time to come home.'

'You'll bring me tomorrow?'

'Of course,' he promised. 'I'll finish early tomorrow night and–'

'No!' she broke in. 'First thing in the morning. I want to be here when Tom and Lucy wake up!'

'Dorrie, you need to get some rest!' he began. 'And I daren't take any more days off–'

'Then I'll come by bus,' she declared, and cast a desperate glance back to the unit. She felt as though she was leaving part of herself behind.

'All right,' Graham relented, because he couldn't think of what else to say. Perhaps Ailsa could persuade her? Women were better at handling this kind of thing. 'I'll bring you on my way to the factory. Just for tomorrow, mind.'

However, Dorrie continued her vigil each and every day after that. She was often alone, because she usually declined Ailsa's offers of company, and Graham was too busy with the Chadwick's contract to spare the time.

Sunlight was streaming into their small kitchen one evening when they were having their meal. It was only the fourth occasion they'd eaten together since Dorrie had been discharged from hospital, and Graham watched in dismay as she listlessly pushed the food around her plate, not touching a bite.

'Why don't you visit the Hamiltons?' he suggested. 'Ena's always asking you.'

'I'd rather not,' she replied quickly, and as swiftly changed the subject. 'I've filled some rolls, and there's cold pie for your supper.' Dorrie set the dishes on the drainer and fetched a plastic box from the fridge. 'Will you be very late again?'

'Ay, don't wait up.'

Provided he pressed on, there was a slim chance he'd finish the Chadwick's job on time – which meant he would avoid the hefty penalty written into the contract.

Thoughtfully he took the sandwich box from Dorrie.

'Shall I walk you over to the hall?' he suggested. 'Ailsa and the others would be glad of an extra pair of hands. It'd be better than you sitting here on your own.'

Dorrie shook her head. 'I don't want to go out in case the hospital rings,' she said simply. 'I'll just stay here and finish my sewing.'

Instead of driving straight to Chadwick's, as he had planned, on impulse Graham stopped off at the village hall where Ailsa was busy with last-minute preparations for the WI bring-and-buy sale.

He sought her out and drew her aside.

'All this waiting and watching Dorrie's doing at the hospital – and her never setting foot outside the house because they might phone… It's got to stop!' he declared, struggling to keep his voice low in the crowded hall. 'It's not right! I thought you would've talked to her – made her see sense!'

'Sense?' Ailsa felt impatience rising, but reminded herself that Graham was young and under a lot of pressure. 'Dorrie's heart and mind will be at that hospital until her babies are home where they belong,' she continued evenly. 'She's sure that being with Tom and Lucy helps them – and she's probably right. Any mother would feel the same!'

The house was in darkness when Graham got in late that night.

In spite of his worries he fell into a heavy, dreamless sleep the instant his head touched the pillow.

He wasn't certain what had wakened him an hour or so later. Weary and disorientated, it was a moment or two before he realised that Dorrie wasn't beside him.

What if there had been a phone call…?

Stumbling from bed, he went out on to the landing and stood for a moment, listening. Everywhere quiet. No lights.

Then he noticed the door at the end of the landing was ajar.

He found Dorrie sitting in the darkness of the empty nursery, her head bowed, her hands folded. The cot quilt she'd embroidered for the twins was spread across her knees.

Seeing her like this made something inside snap.

'For pity's sake, Dorrie – it's the middle of the night! What do you think you're doing?'

'Just sitting – thinking,' she replied sorrowfully. 'Since I've had my own babies, I think about Isobel all the more. Being separated from your children is a terrible thing.'

'This is–' Words failed him, and he shook his head despairingly. 'Dorrie, carrying on like this isn't going to help anybody. Not you – or the twins.'

'You don't understand! You're never here!' she cried accusingly, getting up and turning her back on him. 'You hardly ever visit Tom and Lucy. You haven't seen the way Tom's getting stronger each day – but Lucy's still so tiny! You've no idea what it's like to watch her – she depends on that machine to even breathe!' Dorrie's voice was rising in her distress. 'Every time I leave her, I think I might never see her again. You just don't understand, Graham,' she repeated. 'You don't know what it's like losing a baby!'

Graham felt as though he had been slapped across the face.

'Don't I?' he murmured in a voice that was scarcely audible.

'It's not the same!' she cried, shivering despite the warmth of the summer night. 'It's – it's different!'

'Ay, maybe it is.' He forced himself to speak for the very first time of the child they had lost when Dorrie had miscarried. 'But he was my son, too!' he whispered.

Graham had been at Chadwick's since before five that morning, and as he drove home for an early lunch, he was preoccupied with calculating the amount of work still to be done.

Turning into the drive, he hardly noticed Ailsa scurrying from the house.

'Can't stop! I'm off for the bus!' she called as he drew up.

He nodded absently as he switched off the engine, and went indoors.

Dorrie was in the living-room, sitting at the table checking through the account books.

'How are the twins?' he asked at once. 'Is everything still all right?'

Dorrie nodded. 'Lucy had put on a wee bit when Dr Phipps weighed her. Otherwise she's about the same.' She smiled up at him wistfully. 'But Tom really beamed at me! I told him we'd be bringing him home this afternoon and it was as if he understood!'

As emotion overcame him Graham shut his eyes tightly for a few seconds. When he opened them again, he bent to kiss Dorrie's forehead before sinking heavily into one of the armchairs.

'I'll collect you in plenty of time for us to get over to the hospital. It's four-thirty, isn't it?'

'Yes.' She sorted through the papers set out into neat stacks on the table before her. 'A cheque from Mr and Mrs Cronin came this morning – for their bathroom and kitchen.'

'It's about time they coughed up,' he returned.

'This came in the post, too.' She fingered several typewritten sheets. 'It's from the finance company,' she went on hesitantly. 'If you don't clear the arrears and bring your account up to date within seven days, they – they're going to repossess the van.'

He stared at the documents, but didn't attempt to take them.

'That's the last straw.' He expelled a long breath. 'I've been worrying about it for months, and now it's finally happened.' He shook his head helplessly. 'I haven't the money to pay them.'

'There's the Cronins' cheque,' Dorrie declared.

'It's nothing like enough,' he returned. 'And without the van, I can't work.' He rubbed a hand wearily across his eyes. 'It'd be best if I pack up the business now and start looking for a job before I get any deeper into debt.'

'You can't just give up!' she exclaimed, aghast. 'We'll make economies. Manage somehow!'

'It's no use.' He met her eyes, shame and regret shadowing his. 'I'm so sorry. I wanted so much for us – had such grand plans – but all I've done is let you down.'

'Don't think like that!' she cried. 'You've worked as hard as anybody could and you haven't let me down. But you'll be letting yourself down if you just sit around feeling sorry for yourself and talking about giving up. What about Chadwick's? That's a good contract. Once they pay you, things'll start looking up.'

He shook his head again. 'Even though I've been putting in extra hours, there's no way I'll finish on time. It's too much work for one man,' he explained dismally. 'And I certainly can't afford to hire somebody.'

'No…' Dorrie hesitated as an idea came to her. 'What about Jim?' she suggested in a rush. 'Perhaps he'd help you out!'

'Jim?' he echoed in disbelief at the mention of his elder brother. 'We've not seen him since Mum's funeral! Jim wouldn't give me the time of day – and I wouldn't ask him!'

'Don't be so hasty!' she argued in exasperation. 'You haven't talked to him in years. How do you know what he'd do? Look, Graham, you're fighting to save your business. *Our future.* Surely it wouldn't do any harm to get in touch with him?' she persisted. 'After all, you're family!'

'You don't realise what you're saying. We were never close – not like you and your sisters.' He got up, pacing the room. 'You don't know the bitterness between us. I'd lose everything before I'd ask him for a favour!'

'I don't see that you have any choice!' Dorrie exclaimed, infuriated by his obstinacy. 'Your brother surely won't hold a grudge over something that happened when you were seventeen!'

'Dorrie, I walked out when the family was in trouble,' Graham muttered, glowering at her. 'I can't – won't – ask for help now I'm in the same boat.'

'But you'll end up in court if you don't find some money. And you can't finish Chadwick's on time without help–' Dorrie broke off as the cooker timer buzzed.

'We have Tom and Lucy to think of now,' she concluded briskly, two bright patches staining her cheeks as she started for the kitchen. 'They're more important than old grievances.'

Her hands were unsteady as she drew the casserole out of the oven, and she almost dropped it as Ailsa rapped at the glass of the back door.

She slid the dish onto a trivet on the table and unlocked the door.

'Mum! Where did you rush off to?'

'Town. Got into the main post office just before closing!' she explained breathlessly, her pleased expression changing to concern at Dorrie's tense face. 'What is it? There's not been bad news from the hospital? Or about Isobel...?'

'Oh, no! Nothing like that, thank heavens,' Dorrie interrupted hurriedly. 'But – Graham and I had words.'

'You'd better give him this then.' Ailsa passed her a brown envelope.

'Your savings!' Dorrie exclaimed, looking

inside. 'We can't!'

'Yes, you can. You must.'

'Oh, Mum...' she whispered gratefully. 'Graham'll be so relieved. But you must give it to him!'

With Dorrie at her heels, Ailsa went into the living-room where Graham was slumped at the table, trying to absorb the legal language of the finance company's notice.

'It isn't much,' Ailsa began quietly, sliding the envelope on to the table. 'But it'll bring the van payments up to date – and there should be enough left to tide you over until you get paid for the canteen. I only wish it could be more,' she finished, touching his shoulder sympathetically.

'I don't want your money!' Graham exploded, almost knocking over the chair as he got to his feet. 'It's bad enough that I can't provide for my wife and family, without taking hand-outs from my mother-in-law!'

He thrust the envelope back at Ailsa and strode past her to the door.

With a shocked glance at her mother, Dorrie went after him into the hall.

'What's the matter with you?'

'I still have my pride if nothing else!' He grabbed his jacket and wrenched open the front door. 'Can't you understand that?'

'Graham!' she called, following as he marched away down the path. 'Where are you going?'

'To work – for all the good it'll do!' he shouted over his shoulder, unlocking the van. 'I'll be back about four.'

'Wait!' she cried, but the telephone began to ring, freezing her in her tracks.

She hesitated as the van's noisy engine fired, then turned and half-ran indoors, a familiar fear clutching at her heart as she snatched up the receiver.

'Dr Phipps! What is it?' Dorrie demanded, instantly recognising the other woman's voice. 'Is something wrong?'

Graham got as far as the factory gates before the impact of what had happened hit him. How could he have rowed with Dorrie at a time like this? And throwing Ailsa's kindness back in her face like that!

What had he been thinking of? Suddenly everything seemed to overwhelm him...

Starting up the van again, he drove aimlessly around town before making for the loch where he and Dorrie had often walked when they were courting, and there he sat for the rest of the afternoon.

He was in a much calmer frame of mind by the time he headed home. He expected to find Dorrie and Ailsa rushing around getting ready to go to the hospital to collect Tom. But the house was quiet and empty...

It was then he remembered the phone ringing as he'd driven away. What if it had been the hospital? Suppose Tom's tests hadn't–

'Graham? Is that you?' Dorrie's voice drifted downstairs. 'Can you come up?'

He took the stairs two at a time.

'Dorrie, what's–' But then he halted there on the landing, staring through into the nursery.

Dorrie was standing in the gaily decorated room, her face wreathed in smiles as she cradled Tom in her arms.

'Look, Tom!' she whispered, her eyes never leaving Graham's face. 'Look – your daddy's home.'

Graham stared at his wife and his son. He had never confessed it to Dorrie, but there had been occasions when he had almost given up hope that this day would ever come.

'Don't you want to hold him?' Dorrie smiled, raising the drowsy baby to his arms. 'Don't be afraid to cuddle him. He won't break!'

Graham just nodded, and with the child nestled in his arms he let Dorrie steer him to the rocking-chair. Tom's wide blue eyes fluttered open and then closed again, as he snuggled deeper into Graham's jumper.

'Is he all right?' he asked anxiously. 'He seems awfully still.'

'He's just been fed. He's sleepy.' Dorrie perched on the edge of the ottoman to watch the two of them together. 'He'll probably be wide awake all night and keep us up!'

'I won't mind,' Graham said gruffly, beginning to rock in the chair, his gaze never leaving Tom's face.

When he did glance up, he saw Dorrie's eyes were wet.

'I wish Lucy was home, too,' she whispered.

'She will be soon,' he returned.

'It was dreadful having to leave her behind this afternoon,' Dorrie went on brokenly. 'She was watching us. When she saw us taking Tom, she started to cry – I asked Mum to stay with her.' She swallowed the sob, reaching out to touch Tom's tiny, curled fingers. 'I didn't want her to feel we were abandoning her.'

'She'll be all right,' Graham persisted, frowning with concern. Dorrie wasn't like herself. She'd never been weepy like this before the twins were born. 'She's getting stronger every day, you know that.'

'How come you brought Tom home early?' he asked after a minute, deliberately changing the subject.

'Dr Phipps had to stand in for a colleague at the clinic this afternoon. She asked if we'd collect Tom after lunch,' Dorrie explained absently, tucking the shawl Isobel had crocheted more snugly around Tom's toes. 'I phoned Chadwick's, but you weren't there.'

'I ended up out at the loch. Everything seemed such a mess. I just didn't know what to do for the best, but...' His gaze slid from her to Tom, and across to the two cradles he'd made. 'Is Ailsa still willing to lend me that money–?'

'She wouldn't take it back,' Dorrie returned softly. 'It's in the bureau.'

'It'll only be a loan,' he insisted. 'I'll repay every penny as soon as I can.'

Dorrie glanced at him questioningly and he went on, 'I'm not giving up – at least, not till I've talked to Jim. You were right. There's no-one else can possibly help.' He sighed. 'Did I ever tell you what happened? Exactly what happened...?'

Dorrie said nothing, realising this was

hard for Graham to talk about.

'The croft's been in our family for generations. Mum and Dad loved the land – but Jim and I didn't. We both wanted a different kind of life. Jim had plans to become a builder. Me – I just wanted to get away.

'By the time I left school, Mum and Dad were getting on. Dad's health wasn't good and Jim had already given up his job to help at the croft. He wanted me to stay so we could work together – make something of the place.

'I hated the very idea and – well, as soon as I got fixed up with a job, I just upped and left Jim to it.'

Dorrie covered his hand with her own.

'I wish you'd told me this before.'

'Jim had no choice,' Graham related bleakly. 'He took care of Mum and Dad, and looked after the croft...' He shook his head regretfully. 'I should have stayed. At least until things sorted themselves out.'

'Well, in spite of all that, I think you should get in touch with him again,' Dorrie murmured. 'If for no other reason than to tell him he has a niece and nephew. Family's a precious thing. We can't afford to lose sight of that.'

'I suppose I could write and explain things.'

Graham sighed, unsure how to begin bridging the last eight years. 'Tell him I'll be up to see him. Although I'll not blame him if he tells me to get lost!'

Graham got no answer at the crofthouse door when he arrived at Kincarron the following Friday. Pushing his hands into his pockets, he wandered across the cobbled yard, glad to stretch his legs after the drive and curious to look around.

The place was much as he remembered. Shabbier, though. The croft obviously hadn't been worked for years, and the stone byre was partially converted into a two-storey house.

He was peering inside through one of the grimy windows when he heard a car approaching and he turned round to see Jim Nicholson turning into the yard at the wheel of a taxi.

'So you're a cabby now,' was the only thing Graham could think of saying as his elder brother strode towards him. 'You'll be working mostly in Inverness?'

'Beats this place,' Jim replied dourly. 'I'm my own boss – but it could be better. You look well enough,' he continued, starting past Graham to the crofthouse. 'And your wife and family?'

'Doing fine. Tom's settled in a treat at home, and we expect Lucy out of hospital soon,' Graham responded enthusiastically. 'What about yourself?' he asked as he followed Jim indoors. 'Are you wed?'

'I was going to be – remember Moira Ross? She and I were engaged. But that was years ago, when Mum and Dad were still alive. Moira wanted me to leave the croft and move to town but I...' Jim hesitated, as though he'd already said far more than he'd intended. 'Look, what's past is past, Graham. It's the future we have to look to. There's no sense in beating about the bush. You need my help to finish your factory job, and I need an extra pair of hands up here. I've had to sell off most of the land, so there's only this house and the byre left. I'm doing them up to sell them.' He took a key from the hook by the door. 'Come outside and I'll show you how far I've got.'

'You're talking about months of work!' Graham exclaimed once he had considered the stone byre half an hour later. 'Granted, between us, we've tackled most kinds of jobs, but we're not builders, Jim. Or architects.'

'The specialised work's all been done. The conversion only needs finishing off,' Jim argued impatiently. 'What do you say?'

'But it'd mean me living up here. Being away from home,' Graham hedged desperately, his mind back at Auchlanrick with Dorrie and the children. 'Be reasonable, man. I've a young family to think about!'

'My labour now – for yours later.' Jim faced his brother in the byre's dim light. 'That's my offer. Take it or leave it.'

Chapter Ten

A Bizarre Nightmare

The days since Ortega's troops had commandeered the train had settled into a peculiarly orderly pattern. Travelling around the clock, they steamed farther and farther away from the border and back towards the capital city.

Routine stops were made for fuel and water and for local people to get on and off.

Although heavily armed, the soldiers paid little attention to their passengers. Douglas, Isobel and the others could easily have slipped away from the train – if they'd had the energy to do so.

Instead, Isobel wearily tended the wounded soldiers, while Angela and Luis rarely emerged from the boxcar where Cesar Bernaldez was resting. The frail old man sometimes didn't even recognise them as they tried to make him as comfortable as the oppressive heat and the train's lurching motion allowed.

'Just because none of them is over twenty doesn't mean you can get careless, Karl,' Sam remonstrated as they clambered aboard the train after taking on coal. 'Mentioning Luis like that! It's lucky that kid didn't understand a word of English.'

He cast a backward glance to where the soldiers in their untidy uniforms were sauntering about the rail-stop, drinking beer and smoking cheap cigars, but none of them seemed to have noticed anything untoward.

'It was a slip of the tongue, OK?' the professor retorted irritably.

He sank heavily on to one of the wooden seats and watched Angela pass along the corridor for a breath of air. She practically ignored him these days, spending all her time with Luis Rosales.

'Karl – are you listening? Right now, these lads haven't a clue who we are,' Sam persisted testily. 'But they've watched their friends die and they're scared and bitter. There's no guessing what they'd do – to all of us – if they find out the only son of their enemy is one of us–' He broke off, his attention caught by Luis's sudden appearance in the corridor.

Although less than five yards away, Luis walked blindly past them and straight to Angela.

'He's dead, Angelina,' he said quietly.

'Oh, no,' she whispered. It wasn't unexpected, but... She reached up, touching his ashen face. 'I'm so very sorry.'

'Cesar...' Luis faltered, sorrow constricting his throat. 'He was thirsty. I went for water. I was gone only for a few minutes, but when I went back–'

'My condolences for your loss,' Sam interrupted brusquely, stepping forward. 'But now you must concentrate on saving your own life. We'll say nothing about Cesar's death until the train's about to pull out. By then the soldiers will have drunk enough to be amenable,' he concluded calmly. 'Staying here overnight to arrange the funeral will give you plenty of time to get away.'

'No!' Luis exclaimed, his hand clasping Angela's. 'I wish to attend Cesar's burial.

And what about Angelina? Or do you believe I'm a coward–'

'You still don't get it, do you, Luis?' Sam cut in bluntly. 'You're a danger to the rest of us.'

'He's right, Luis,' Angela urged gently. 'When we get to Castildoro and give ourselves up, it'll go easier for us if they think we haven't seen you since the plane crash. You've been wanting to fight for your country's freedom, so go and do it!'

'We should all go.' Luis glanced sombrely from her to Sam and the others.

'We'd never make it,' Douglas replied simply. 'And I'm not sure how much more Isobel can take.'

After a moment, Luis inclined his head in acceptance.

'I'd like to be with Cesar for a while. Excuse me.' He turned, and Angela immediately went after him, linking her fingers through his.

None of the three men spoke immediately. Cesar Bernaldez's death had touched each of them.

'You should go, too,' Douglas said unexpectedly, glancing at Sam. 'Enrique Soler said they're looking for you, too. Ortega would love to make an example of you. This could be your only chance of staying alive.'

Three days after Cesar Bernaldez's burial, the train approached a sizeable town. As Douglas, who was driving the train, braked to draw alongside the station, he saw an army Jeep, flanked by armed motor-cyclists, waiting on the dusty timber platform.

'Reception committee. None other than Enrique Soler,' he announced over his shoulder to Karl. 'Fetch Isobel and Angie up here. I don't want them alone when the troops board.'

Soler jumped from the Jeep, signalling for Douglas and the others to alight. When they were lined up on the platform, he grinned humourlessly.

'Destiny is indeed capricious, Dr Blundell. Our paths continually cross. Get in.' He indicated the Jeep. 'I have orders to take your party directly to General Ortega.'

'We're British and US civilians,' Douglas protested, well aware that it was futile. 'You have no authority over us.'

Soler raised his shoulders in an indifferent gesture, indicating the armed troops.

'I believe I have all the authority necessary. Come quickly, please. General Ortega is not a patient man.'

With no choice but to comply they climbed into the Jeep and sat, two facing two, on the benches in its open rear section.

While Soler drove, the soldier in the passenger seat turned to watch them.

The Jeep gathered speed, pulling clear of the station with the motor-cyclists riding parallel at either side. Isobel sat hunched beside Douglas, her eyes downcast. He gripped her limp hand.

'Don't worry,' he said, trying to brace her. 'They're just trying to intimidate us.'

Karl Fischer leaned forward to ensure his words couldn't be overheard. 'I wonder how Sam and Luis are doing?'

'They'll have made it!' Angela murmured decisively. 'Luis knows the mountains very well. Oh, my Lord – look!'

As Soler swung down the curving road into the outskirts of Castildoro, evidence lay everywhere of the fierce struggle which had taken place in the sleepy city before it had finally fallen to Ortega. Houses were razed, whole blocks burned out and abandoned. Two bullet-pitted tanks had been abandoned close to the church gardens and farther ahead the rubble of the bank was crumpled into a gaping crater.

'Where is everybody?' Karl Fischer asked.

The streets were deserted, except for patrols of soldiers in grimy battledress green.

Soler shrugged. 'Castildoro has a strictly enforced curfew.'

Government House had been taken over as the military headquarters, but Soler drove past the imposing building.

Increasing speed, he left the city behind and headed out into the rolling countryside beyond. Eventually Angela recognised the route.

'This leads to Casa Rey!' she exclaimed. 'I've spent vacations there. The owners are friends of my parents.'

'That's quite correct, Miss Lennard.' Soler glanced at her in the rear-view mirror. 'The hacienda was for many generations the summer home of the Aragall family. General Ortega has established his personal household at Casa Rey.'

'Then what's happened to Señor Aragall and his wife?' Angela demanded. 'Where are they?'

'In prison,' Soler responded unemotionally, as the lights of the hacienda glimmered between strands of shadowy trees.

The Jeep, with its escort of motor-cyclists, passed between ornate iron gates into a courtyard heavy with the scent of oleander and thickly fringed with magnolia trees. As it drew alongside an elegant arcade, a tall, distinguished man emerged from the tiled portico.

'Good evening! I am Gualterio Ortega. Welcome to Casa Rey,' he greeted them graciously. 'Please, come inside...'

They stepped into a cool, marble-paved hall. Its walls were of extravagantly carved red mahogany and soft lamplight spilled from numerous niches and alcoves. Classical music was drifting through the open doors of the library, and hovering in an archway beyond the sweeping staircase was a small, middle-aged woman dressed entirely in black.

'Febe will show you to your rooms. Naturally you will wish to rest and clean up. Perhaps later, you will join me for dinner?' Ortega continued. 'Meanwhile, if you require anything, do not hesitate to ring. I'm most anxious that your stay at Casa Rey be as pleasant as possible.'

There wasn't anything they could do but follow the housekeeper up the imposing staircase.

Febe paused at one of the doors and pushed it wide.

'Dr and Mrs Blundell, this is your room.'

She flicked a switch and lamps sprang alight on the cream-washed walls to illuminate the spacious bedroom with its tall, shuttered windows.

'I will bring you some tea directly,' she added, then withdrew to escort the others to their rooms.

Despite the circumstances, Isobel gasped in incredulous wonder as her gaze swept over the exquisite tapestries and hand-woven rugs, the painted ceiling, the graceful Spanish renaissance furniture and damask-upholstered chairs...

After everything they'd been through, to have finally come face to face with the man they so feared, and to find themselves surrounded by such beauty and opulence, was like a scene from some bizarre nightmare where nothing made sense.

Her knees buckled and she sank on to the corner of the huge bed.

Then her gaze found the open wardrobe – and she saw that their clothes were hanging inside.

'Douglas...' she mumbled, getting up to run her hands over the dresses and skirts. 'I don't understand. These things – they're ours! We had to leave them behind. How did he get them?'

'From the plane wreckage, I suppose.' Douglas frowned, his comforting arms about her. 'Ortega's obviously gone to a great deal of trouble to arrange this. I wonder why? What's he up to, Izzie?'

He wasn't to find out until much later that evening.

He and Isobel had bathed and changed and Febe had brought the promised tray of tea. He had persuaded Isobel to rest and was sitting beside her while she slept when Febe noiselessly returned to tell him that his presence was required in the library.

The music was still playing, strident and bellicose now, but tuned to a low volume.

'Ah, Dr Blundell!' Ortega exclaimed genially, glancing around from the drinks cabinet. 'I adore Wagner, don't you?'

'Not particularly,' Douglas retorted, distractedly waving aside the sherry Ortega was offering and meeting the man's eyes with a steady gaze. 'Just get to the point, will you? Why have you brought us here? What do you want from us?'

'He's coming from Paris at midnight?' Janey sighed, watching Kirsty fussing around making the spare room ready. 'That's really romantic!'

'Josh is a romantic man,' Kirsty commented with satisfaction, her eyes sparkling as she put a gift-wrapped bottle of his favourite aftershave on to the pile of clean towels in the dresser drawer. 'I'm delighted to say!'

'Of course, he's half Italian,' Janey mused. 'And Latins are very passionate...'

'Is that right?' Kirsty inquired, lightly flicking Janey's thick fringe with her fingertips as they started downstairs. 'I'll have to take your word for it, miss! Actually, I'm a bit nervous about this weekend,' she confided candidly. 'Josh and I lead such different lives now. It's months since we saw one another. What if we've changed...?'

The back door burst open and Teddy began barking ecstatically. There was a clamour of excited voices and running feet and paws came thundering along the hall.

'Oh, no! Paul and the boys are back already!' Janey groaned. 'I wanted you to help me with my hair!'

'I still will,' Kirsty promised, jumping down the last few stairs to be instantly surrounded. 'How's the newspaper business, boys?'

'The printer let me press the button!' Robbie shouted, tugging on her sleeve, his

213

chubby face upturned. 'We put the paper to bed!'

'That's newsroom talk,' Paul explained with a grin.

'I know that!' she returned airily, but her eyes were grave when they met Paul's above the boys' heads.

He'd promised to contact the Foreign Office again today, and Kirsty's spirits plummeted at his slight, negative gesture. She bent to put her arms about both Alasdair and Robbie's shoulders.

'There's some milk and Mrs Bell's toffee buns waiting for you in the kitchen. But only one each, mind. Save the rest for your camp-out this evening.'

As the boys scampered off, she straightened to find Paul watching her and smiling. The warmth in his eyes took her by surprise.

'What?'

'Nothing.' He shrugged, still smiling at her and thinking, not for the first time, how much she had changed recently. She looked so right now with the family gathered around her. 'Oh, I almost forgot,' he announced suddenly, and began patting the pockets of his jacket as he tried to remember where he had put something. 'We met the postman in the lane. Package for you. I had to sign for it, so it must be important.'

'I'm not expecting anything.' She took the padded bag and scrutinised it.

'Hurry and open it!' Janey urged. 'It might be a present!'

Laughing at the girl's impatience, Kirsty tugged open the end of the packet and peered in.

'Oh, that's nice!' she exclaimed. 'It's a complimentary copy of Wuthering Heights, the audio novel I narrated for Josh's recording company!' Her face lit up as she turned it over in her hands. 'Doesn't it look smart?'

'Mmm, very nice,' Paul commented. 'My mother adores the Brontës. She's in the Society at Haworth,' he added.

'Kirsty could've played Cathy on TV!' Janey announced rather grandly. 'Her agent said the boss of a big new series wanted her to be the star.'

'Well, not quite,' Kirsty cautioned, and went on to explain: 'They're planning a serial of Wuthering Heights. Apparently the producer heard an advance copy of this–' she tapped the audio novel '–and knew my theatre work, and he approached Ruth, my agent. I probably wouldn't have actually got the part.'

'Bet you would!' Janey declared loyally, starting back upstairs again. 'I'll go and wash my hair.'

'OK. Give me a shout when you're ready.' Kirsty moved toward the kitchen, glancing at Paul. 'Can I get you a coffee, or do you have to get back to the paper?'

'Yes, please. And no, I don't have to get back. What's the point of being the boss if you can't play truant occasionally?' he replied. 'Kirsty, before we join the boys,' he added hurriedly, 'would you like to visit Haworth? It's a fascinating place, and I'd enjoy showing you around.'

'That would be nice,' she answered, carefully keeping the tone light. 'Isn't there a railway museum nearby? Alasdair and Robbie'd like that. And you never know, exploring the Brontës' home might even inspire Janey to read a book!'

'We can turn it into a family trip, by all means,' he agreed. 'But, if Winifred Bell will mind the children, I'd rather hoped you and I might have a day out. Just the two of us.'

'I couldn't do that,' she said softly. 'Paul, I know that in many ways we're closer than ever before, but you have to understand that Josh is the most important person in my life just now.'

He shook his head, meeting her eyes with thinly disguised exasperation.

'You're too impulsive. Too emotional. Everything's always all or nothing with you. And quite frankly,' he added for ill-advised good measure, 'I think you're far more committed to the relationship than he is!'

Even as the words spilled out of his mouth he knew it was the worst possible moment to have this out with her. But he couldn't now leave unsaid what had been in his mind for weeks so he blundered on.

'If Josh Elliott loved you as much as you think – hope – he does, he wouldn't have gone abroad and left you when you needed him most.'

Kirsty was stunned by his bluntness.

'That's not fair!' she protested. 'Josh has a career to think of!'

'*You* had a career,' he countered, 'but you gave it up when the people you love needed you.'

'Mine was a different situation entirely,' Kirsty returned. 'Opportunities were opening up at the Paris studios for Josh. He would have been crazy to turn them down.'

'Not in my view,' Paul countered. 'All right, so his staying in Britain might have meant a sideways career move, but he could have done it – if he'd wanted to! Look, if I've upset you, I'm sorry,' he concluded regretfully, his attitude softening, 'but I want you to see things as they are – not as you want them to be!'

With the exception of Janey – who scorned camping-out when you were only pitching your tent in the garden – the family spent that afternoon wandering back and forth with all the necessaries for Paul and the boys' forthcoming night under canvas.

Paul himself was in the cellars, searching for a missing piece of the camping stove, when the ring of the telephone brought him up for air.

'Kirsty!' he yelled from the garden doorway, beckoning her up from the riverbank. 'Phone!'

'Is it Paris?' she queried breathlessly, sprinting indoors. 'Josh?'

He nodded and disappeared back down to the cellar.

'Josh? I just knew it would be you,' she began, almost shyly. 'Only seven-and-a-bit hours to go!'

'We're having nothing but problems here, sweetheart,' he said without preamble. 'There's no way I'll make my flight this evening. Sorry.'

Usually they'd talk for hours, but suddenly there seemed nothing left to say. Besides, he had to get back into the studio, he said.

Kirsty held on to the receiver long after the line from Paris had gone dead until suddenly she became aware that Paul was standing beside her.

'I couldn't help overhearing,' he murmured awkwardly, stretching out a hand to touch her shoulder, then withdrawing. 'I know you were looking forward...' The sentence tailed off and he paused, studying the stove he was holding. 'I can see to the boys, if you want.'

'No. I – I'm all right. Thanks, anyway,' she faltered. Paul's sympathy was far more upsetting than his criticism. 'I'll be out in a minute.'

He nodded again, and walked along the hall to the garden.

Kirsty squeezed her eyes tightly shut and expelled a ragged breath, disappointment and apprehension mixing in the pit of her stomach. Josh wasn't coming tonight. And he hadn't said when – or if – he *would* be coming.

As it was already arranged for Winifred to

watch over things next day, Kirsty decided to spend her unexpected free time usefully and caught the early train to collect the remainder of her belongings from the London flat she, Josh, and Gwen Howells had shared.

Gwen was still dancing in summer season at Rhyl and, although they got along well enough, Kirsty was relieved that she wouldn't be seeing her flatmate. She wasn't up to fending off her chatty inquisitiveness, especially where Josh was concerned.

Wearily she climbed the three flights from the street. Although the flat wasn't as comfortable, or as cosy, as the wee house at Auchlanrick, it was her home, and giving it up was painful. From now on she wouldn't have anywhere to really call her own. The last piece of her independence was gone.

She was about to put her key into the lock when the door swung open and Gwen and Josh stood framed in the doorway.

They looked as astonished to see her as Kirsty was to see them.

She took an involuntary step backwards, noticing that Josh was freshly shaven, the ends of his hair damp from the shower.

'Kirsty!' he exclaimed, recovering first. 'Gwen and I were going for breakfast–'

'Reckon I ought to make myself scarce!' Gwen chuckled, kissing Kirsty's cheek. 'Lovely to see you. Shame you have to give up your room. It's rotten luck. See you later!'

Josh drew Kirsty into the flat and closed the door behind them, catching Kirsty's sleeve when she would've walked straight past him into the lounge.

'Darling...' he murmured, drawing her back against him and circling her with his arms, his lips unerringly locating the racing pulsebeat at the base of her throat.

Kirsty stood rigid, numb inside, unable to return the warmth of Josh's caresses.

'What's wrong?' he asked.

'Nothing.'

'Nothing?' he echoed sceptically, searching her eyes. 'I know you too well to believe that.'

'I – I'm just surprised to see you here,' she managed to stammer, alarmed at the direction her thoughts were taking. 'And Gwen.'

'She's in town for a pantomime audition–' He broke off, then continued with sudden realisation. 'That's it, isn't it? It's Gwen! You think she and I–'

'No!' Kirsty protested untruthfully, averting her eyes and trying to pull free, but

Josh's strong hands were still gripping her arms. 'I don't think that!'

'Of course you do!' he retorted in disgust, finally setting her free. 'It's written all over your face.'

'Well – what am I supposed to think?' she retaliated. 'You told me you had to stay in Paris!'

'I *was* in Paris. We worked all night and I got the first plane back this morning. There was nothing directly into Leeds, so– Oh, what's the point?' he demanded. 'Trust should run both ways, Kirsty.'

'What's that supposed to mean?' she challenged.

'You see me with Gwen and immediately suspect the worst,' he retorted bitterly, 'yet for months I've had to accept the fact you've been seeing more of your ex-boyfriend than you have of me. Whenever you phone or write, it's "Paul said this" or "Paul did that"!'

'He's the children's godfather,' Kirsty pointed out coldly. 'He comes to see them, not me!'

Josh shook his head. 'Get a grip on reality, Kirsty. Anyone can see the man still loves you.'

'That's nonsense!' she snapped. 'Paul's a

fine man and he's a friend! Nothing more.'

'Are you absolutely sure about that?' he countered.

Pointedly not answering and breaking their eye contact, Kirsty turned towards her room.

'I'll fetch my things. That's why I came.'

He leaned against the door frame, watching her.

'You've a lot of stuff. Why not leave half of it in my room?' he suggested with brittle politeness. 'Collect it next time you're down.'

'I won't be coming here again.' Kirsty didn't look at him nor pause from frantically pushing her belongings into bags. She was desperate just to get away from him, to get out of the flat, to be on her way home...

'If that's how you want it,' Josh commented evenly, his quietness more disturbing than anger. 'Run back to him. I'll even drive you to Euston!'

'There's no need–'

'Oh, but there's every need.' He stepped forward to grasp her wrist, forcing her to stop her frantic packing. 'I'm not about to make it easy for you. I want you to stop and think!'

She drew breath to reply, but words

wouldn't come. His eyes were staring into hers, and Kirsty saw exactly what Josh was remembering. That other time he'd taken her to the station – and kissed her for the first time...

She blinked hard, lowering her head, remembering the vivid emotions that kiss had stirred.

'What's the matter?' Josh demanded, dragging her closer, forcing her to look up at him. 'Memories too tough to face? Surely not!'

His mouth came down hard upon hers for an instant, then he released her and turned on his heel.

'Let's go. You don't want to miss your train!' he muttered, and snatching up her luggage he strode out.

Kirsty heard the flat's door slam. He was gone. She'd lost him. It was over.

Standing alone in the silence of her old room, the tears she'd earlier denied streamed unnoticed from her eyes.

After they'd explored the old church and museum at Haworth, Paul took the boys for ice-cream at the village tearoom while Kirsty and Janey lingered at the Brontë house.

They strolled down the straight, neatly-edged path, then paused at the gate to look at the square stone parsonage, where Charlotte, Emily and Anne had spent much of their short lives.

'Funny to think of them sitting in that little parlour writing their books, isn't it?' Janey murmured, smoothing her fingers across the copy of Wuthering Heights she'd just bought from the shop. 'You seemed miles away when we were looking around. Were you thinking about playing Cathy?'

'A little,' Kirsty admitted, as they turned the church corner and started down the steep, cobbled street to the village. 'But mostly I was thinking about your mum, and Dorrie and me. It's been years since we've all been together with Mum.'

'D'you think Gran'll come back soon to look after us?'

'She can't. She can't leave Dorrie yet,' Kirsty replied simply. 'One new baby takes a lot of looking after, and Dorrie has to decide between caring for Tom at home and being with Lucy at the hospital. So you're stuck with Paul and me!'

Janey laughed, then her eyes clouded.

'There hasn't been any news for ages, has there?'

Kirsty shook her head, and slipped an arm around the teenager's shoulders.

'Paul's always trying to get more information but he hasn't had much luck lately.' She paused. 'It doesn't mean anything's happened – just that news isn't getting out.'

Janey gave a resigned sigh, not speaking again until they were strolling past the Black Bull, when the display in a nearby shop window caught her eye.

'Oh, wouldn't Mum love that!' She pointed to a handmade quilt. 'You know how she likes old-fashioned things!'

They stopped to admire the colourful quilt's traditional patchwork design.

'Do you want it?' Kirsty asked impulsively. 'To give to your mum and dad? From you and Alasdair and Robbie?'

'It's terribly expensive. Can we really have it?' Janey asked, her eyes shining. 'It could be a welcome home present for them, couldn't it? When they come home,' she repeated positively.

'My sentiments exactly!' Kirsty declared, and linking her arm through Janey's she tugged her into the shop.

That evening, Paul came downstairs after seeing both boys into bed and found Kirsty stuffing the day's shorts, socks and T-shirts into the washing machine.

'Fancy a drink?'

'Good idea. There's some white wine in the fridge.'

He filled two tall glasses and took them out to the patio, where she joined him on the comfortable wooden bench there.

'Thanks.' She smiled up at him. 'Are the boys settled?'

'Robbie was asleep before his head touched the pillow. Alasdair's trying to read, but he can hardly keep his eyes open.' Paul chuckled. 'It was a good day, wasn't it?'

'Terrific.' She sighed, drawing a deep, contented breath of the soft, sweet September air. 'It was the perfect way of rounding off their holidays.'

'They did enjoy it, didn't they?' Paul stretched out comfortably, gazing across the vivid heather to Hawksbeard Crag, its ragged edges glowing golden with drying bracken.

'I've always envied Douglas,' he said meditatively. 'Having Isobel and the children. Without a wife and family, a real home and proper roots, true happiness just isn't possible.'

Kirsty glanced at him warily, but his eyes held a faraway expression and he wasn't looking at her.

They sat in companionable silence until the sun dipped beneath the horizon and its afterglow trailed streaks of tangerine, blue and crimson across the sky.

'Robbie asked me if his mum and dad will be back to take him to school,' Kirsty murmured, frowning. 'All the others will have their mums or dads with them on their first day. I'm afraid it'll be upsetting for him.'

'Don't worry. We'll take Robbie to school together, Kirsty. If there are any problems, we'll cope with them. I promised I'd be here for you and the family ... and I will,' he assured her quietly, hesitating before reaching out to smooth a straying wisp of hair from her forehead.

Conscious of the touch of his hand, she met his eyes steadily.

'I'm sorry, Paul. I do like you – in fact, I'm very fond of you – but I can't be more than a friend. I–' She faltered, loth to hurt him, yet wanting to speak plainly so there wouldn't be any misunderstanding. 'I miss Josh so much. Not a single day passes that I don't think about him. It breaks my heart when I think of all we once shared – and everything we've lost.'

Paul held her troubled gaze, his hand light and comforting against her cheek.

'We used to be so much more than friends. I'm sure we could have a happy and contented life– But I realise it's still far too soon for you,' he added quickly. 'I can wait. I asked you to marry me once before, Kirsty. And when the time's right, I'll ask you again.'

Chapter Eleven

Freedom – At A Price!

The days after the children returned to school seemed long and empty for Kirsty. Summer vanished overnight into constant rain and the house even seemed empty and dismal.

Despite the weather, she took to going for long walks along the river in a vain bid to shake off her feelings of isolation and loneliness, and she found herself looking forward keenly to Paul's frequent visits and the days when Winifred Bell came to help with the heavy work.

'I've decided I need to find a part-time job, Win,' she announced one wet Friday when they were baking pies for the harvest festival. 'Do you know of anything?'

''Fraid not. I could ask around, though.'

'I'd be grateful. I've been independent since I was about Janey's age; even a wee job would help. But it really isn't just the money,' she confessed. 'I need to work! I've been so – restless. This is my home now and I honestly thought I'd settled, yet– Oh, I can't even explain it!' She grimaced in exasperation. 'Goodness knows what's come over me. Maybe it's this endless rain and being cooped up on my own day after day. I haven't been right since school started.'

Winifred gave the younger woman a knowing look. When she'd met Paul Ashworth the morning after he'd taken Kirsty and the children to Haworth, he'd recounted every last detail about the outing. And, watching his open, sincere face while he talked, Winifred had understood a great deal more.

'You've not heard from your foreign young man, have you?' she asked unexpectedly.

'Josh? He's not foreign!' Kirsty protested with a giggle. 'Just half Italian. But no, I haven't heard from him,' she added, sobering, 'and I don't expect to. A clean break was the only way.'

'It's funny how things have a habit of turning out for the best,' Winifred remarked evenly. 'You're lucky, Kirsty. You've your whole life still ahead of you. And you haven't to look farther than your own door-step to find a chap who's devoted to you.'

Kirsty half smiled, her eyes lowered as she rolled out the pastry. Paul was in London, harrying his contacts at the Foreign Office again, and she'd been surprised at how much she missed him.

'He tried to warn me about my relation-ship with Josh, you know,' she commented. 'In fact we quarrelled about it. I was sure he was wrong – and I told him so! But in spite of that he's been incredibly understanding these past few months. He's changed since I knew him,' she added thoughtfully. 'Mel-lowed, somehow.'

Winifred paused with her hands elbow deep in the mixing-bowl.

'Happen it's you who's changed, lass. Maybe Paul's been the right one all along, and it's just taken till now for you to realise it.' She nodded approvingly. 'He's a fine man and he loves you dearly. Let him go a second time,' she cautioned, 'and you'll regret it for the rest of your life!'

'Graham's as pleased as Punch about finishing Chadwick's on time and at being able to pay you back so quickly,' Dorrie commented to Ailsa as they cut sandwiches and filled flasks for the brothers' long drive north to Kincarron. 'I know you meant ... oh, Mum, look!'

She was looking through the window to the garden, where Jim had been raking up leaves from the lawn. He had gone across to the twins' pram to retrieve the blanket which Lucy had kicked off and now he was tucking it back gently round them as they slept.

'He's so good with them,' Dorrie murmured affectionately. She'd grown fond of Graham's elder brother and couldn't help feeling that he'd had a rough deal from life. 'I hope he meets somebody nice and has a family of his own some day. He's such a kind man, yet he seems so alone–'

She broke off as Graham came downstairs with his suitcase.

'All set, love?' she asked.

'Just about,' he agreed.

Ailsa wiped her hands on the towel.

'I'll just pop out and tell Jim you're ready to go,' she remarked, and tactfully withdrew.

'Thanks, Ailsa.' Graham returned her

smile, but his expression sobered when he looked at Dorrie. 'You're sure you'll manage while I'm gone?'

'With Tom and Lucy home and getting bigger and bonnier by the day? Of course I will!' she insisted cheerfully. 'Don't worry about us.'

He nodded, and turned away to pull on his jacket.

'I've enjoyed working with Jim again. It was like the old days when we were lads. We were as close as any two brothers could be in those days. I've been thinking about the twins' christening,' he went on hastily, hearing Jim and Ailsa approaching from the garden. 'What d'you think about Jim–'

Dorrie beamed.

'Tom and Lucy couldn't have a finer godfather!' she agreed.

The weather was cold, but dry, and the brothers were outside from first light until dusk. Then they'd go in and work on the interior of the old byre.

Graham put in a few extra hours on the crofthouse, too, taking great pride transforming the dilapidated old dwelling into a pretty cottage.

'We've done all right,' Jim commented,

returning from Inverness late on a sleety November afternoon with a van load of building supplies.

'I've a mind to dig out these cobbles,' Graham responded, shouldering the lengths of wood and striding across the yard from the van. 'With bulbs and suchlike planted, it could be an attractive little garden by spring.'

'There's plenty of space at the back for the sort of vegetable patch Mum had. And for a big family garden, too,' Jim agreed. 'And talking of families – why don't you go home this weekend? Your bairns'll be up and running around if you leave it much longer.'

Graham grinned. 'It has been a while! Are you coming with me?'

'Not this time. I'd better get the taxi out and earn a pound or two to pay for this lot!' Jim replied ruefully. 'Will you and Dorrie be fixing a date for the christening?'

Graham frowned. 'I shouldn't think so. Dorrie's set her heart on waiting until Isobel and Douglas get back from South America. She wants both her sisters there.'

Jim nodded in understanding.

'You can't blame her for that. Has there been any news?'

'Not a word,' Graham replied grimly. 'I've

not said anything to Dorrie, but I can't help wondering if they'll ever get back. Or – or even if they're still alive.'

With that sombre thought hanging over them, the brothers continued unloading the van in near silence, the sleet soaking their hair and clothes. They tramped back and forth across the cobbled yard until Jim finally put into words what he'd been mulling over in his mind for days.

'By rights the croft belongs to both of us. That's the way Mum and Dad would have wanted it. You've put a lot of work into the cottage. If you'd fancy living in it – well, it's a grand place for a family.'

Graham's heart thumped, his dream of providing a home of their very own for Dorrie and the children at odds with what he believed to be fair.

'I'm grateful,' he began quietly. 'But I made my choice nearly eight years ago. Whatever the croft brings is yours – that's only right.'

'The proceeds of selling the byre will be enough for me,' Jim countered. 'And if it's your business you're worried about, Inverness is bound to offer decent prospects for a good painter and decorator.'

Graham didn't answer but he paused in the open doorway, gazing across at the crofthouse's trim roof and neat windows, and sighed. Dorrie would love it, he knew. But would she agree to move from Auchlanrick – leaving her mother alone?

On the spur of the moment, Josh Elliot took the afternoon flight from London to Edinburgh, hired a car, bought a road map and drove north to Auchlanrick.

It was only when he'd actually reached the village and found Ailsa MacFarlane's home that he began to wonder if he was doing the right thing.

However, when he spotted a woman leaving the house with a twin pram he was out of the car in an instant.

'Mrs MacFarlane?' he approached Ailsa at the gate. 'We've never met. I'm Josh Elliot, a – friend of Kirsty's.'

'I know who you are,' she returned stiffly.

Although it wasn't in Kirsty's nature to pour out her heart to her mother, Ailsa was well aware of how badly hurt she had been by this man.

'Nothing's happened, has it?' Ailsa demanded suddenly. 'To Kirsty?'

'What?' Josh queried blankly, momentarily confused. 'No. No. She's fine – as far as I know. I haven't seen or heard from her for several weeks. But she *is* the reason I'm here. Can we talk?'

'I can't invite you inside, I'm afraid,' Ailsa returned, wheeling the pram through the gate and into the lane. 'My daughter had a sleepless night with the babies and she's trying to rest. I don't want her disturbed.'

'Of course.' Josh agreed, and fell into step beside her. 'I only got back to London from Paris this morning, and while I was having lunch I bumped into Ruth Hartman, Kirsty's agent—' He broke off, waiting while Ailsa exchanged a few words with a neighbour, then as they walked on he picked up his story again.

'Mrs MacFarlane, are you aware that there's to be a new TV adaptation of Wuthering Heights?'

'Yes.' She stopped at the pillar-box, checking through several letters before posting them, and Josh did his best to quash his rising irritation at her apparent indifference. 'My granddaughter Janey mentioned something about it,' she added.

Josh nodded. 'Well, according to Ruth Hartman, the serial is casting shortly and both producer and director greatly respect Kirsty's past work, and think she's right to play Cathy.'

His exasperation increased as Ailsa bent to adjust the pram's hood. She scarcely seemed to be listening to a word he was saying!

'Don't you see how important this is?' he pressed on. 'The leading role would almost certainly go to Kirsty – if she tried for it!'

Ailsa finally turned to give him her full attention.

'Kirsty's grown up at last. She's finished with all that acting nonsense!' she snapped. 'She's put down roots, made a proper life for herself–'

'No!' he cut in emphatically, pushing his hand irritably through his hair. 'You just don't understand her at all, do you?' he added, incredulous. 'The only reason Kirsty's left acting is because she has to look after her sister's children.' He sighed. 'Look, I didn't come here to cause trouble. I just want to make sure you realise how much she's having to give up,' he persisted. 'If you went back to Yorkshire, Kirsty would be free–'

'There's no point in discussing it,' Ailsa replied reasonably, turning the pram into the newsagent's. 'Someone has to look after Isobel's children and I can't possibly go. My daughter needs me here.'

'Kirsty's your daughter, too!' Josh's hot temper finally ignited. 'And right now, she's about to make yet another sacrifice for the sake of her family. Think that over, Mrs MacFarlane. You might like to do something about it!'

Douglas leaned back from the computer screen and removed his glasses to massage the bridge of his nose between thumb and forefinger. He'd had no choice; he'd had to accept General Ortega's ultimatum – but that didn't make working for him any less agonising.

The dictator was determined that the excavation at Castildoro should continue, so he needed Douglas's archaeological expertise – along with his contacts amongst private collectors and museums all over the world, for although the Indian, Spanish and Portuguese artefacts being recovered from the site might not be glamorous, they *were* valuable. There was a thriving international black market in such treasures, and selling them would provide finance to arm, feed and clothe Ortega's army.

However, even the general's promise of freedom for Isobel and the others couldn't appease Douglas's conscience.

Despairingly, he rose and crossed the office on the hacienda's ground floor.

Raising the blind, he gazed out across the sunlit garden with its dancing fountain and shady groves of magnolias.

Angela Lennard was strolling along one of the paved paths from the direction of the stables. She was chatting and joking with a small boy as she helped him carry a heavy basket of fresh produce up to the house.

It amazed Douglas how easily she had adapted to captivity at Casa Rey. She hung around the kitchen and stables, gossiping with Febe, the housekeeper, and the other servants, and seemed remarkably content.

On impulse, he strode out into the hot, fragrant garden, and he was standing staring blindly into the fountain when Angela joined him.

'You look awful,' she said. 'And that's being tactful.'

'Thanks,' Douglas replied wryly. 'I saw you earlier. Have you been out riding again?'

'All the way to the electrified fence!' Angela glanced around to see where the nearest guard was. Ortega had kept that part of his promise at least. They were treated as honoured guests, but a member of the general's personal staff was never far away.

Angela bent to the fountain, trailing her fingers idly in the tumbling water.

'Ortega's on his way back. Should be here before dark.'

'How do you know?' Douglas asked, then immediately shook his head apologetically. Angie never revealed where she got her information though he suspected that she had somehow made contact with the local resistance.

'You and the others will be going home, then,' he said instead.

'We'll have to be careful,' she concluded, carelessly playing with the water. 'He's taking heavy losses of men and equipment in the hills, and last night his munitions factory was sabotaged. Douglas, I realise how hard it will be for you, but you must agree to anything – everything – he demands. Don't risk antagonising him,' she concluded, her casual attitude belying the urgency of the warning. 'At best he'll change his mind about sending us home. At worst – he'll kill us!'

Sure enough, the group was told to be ready to leave later that evening, and it was with a heavy heart that Isobel finished packing. She couldn't bear the thought of leaving Douglas.

When her suitcase was ready beside the bedroom door, they stood together, waiting for Febe to knock and tell them it was time to go. A truck would take Isobel and the others to the military airfield.

'Douglas, I promised you – and myself – that, whatever happened, we'd never be separated,' she murmured, her arms folded tightly, as though she were cold. 'If it wasn't for the children, I'd never have agreed–'

'You've got to go.' He kept his tone calm, stroking her hair. 'Once you're home, everything will be back to normal for Janey, Alasdair and Robbie.'

'Normal?' She was aghast. 'Without you?'

'You were due to go home alone after your holiday,' he persisted practically. 'I had another eighteen months work to do. And that's exactly what I'm doing – working,' he concluded. 'I'm useful. Ortega needs me. I'm not in any danger. You have to make the children understand–'

As they heard Febe's soft footsteps approaching along the landing, he drew Isobel into his arms. Although Ortega had granted him permission to see her off at the airfield, these last few moments alone would be precious.

He felt her burrowing her face into his shirt front, knew she was crying, and his own vision blurred.

'Oh, Douglas, I love you…'

He drew her still closer, rubbing his cheek against the softness of her hair. Would this be the very last time he'd ever hold her in his arms...?

Karl, Angela and the other five archaeologists were already seated on timber benches in the windowless rear-section of the military truck when Douglas helped Isobel climb inside.

Hardly a word was exchanged as the heavy vehicle rumbled over rough tracks towards the airfield. Everyone was relieved at being released – but terribly afraid their freedom might be snatched from them at the last moment.

And no-one could forget one of their number would not be boarding the plane – would have to travel back in the empty truck to Casa Rey.

'Isobel, remember – I'll be coming home when this is over,' Douglas whispered against her ear. 'And never forget that I–'

His words were drowned out by a burst of gunfire close to the truck and the heavy vehicle braked violently, lurching and swerving to a juddering stop.

There were more shots and the smashing of glass and wordless shouts, then the truck's rear canvas flap was flung open and a heavily-armed young man wearing camouflage fatigues stood there. His eyes narrowed as he tried to see into the dimness of the vehicle's interior.

'Don't be alarmed, my friends–' His earth-smeared face creased into a white, humourless smile. 'Ortega has stolen much from our country – but now the resistance is doing a little commandeering of its own!'

'Luis!' Angela was first to recover, and almost stumbled from the truck to reach his side. 'I thought you were never coming!'

'You should have had more confidence in us, Angel!'

Sam Fraser strode around from the front of the vehicle. He was wearing the battle-dress green and twin stars of Ortega's generals and paused at the truck's rear to consider its startled, silent passengers.

'Lost for words, Dr Blundell? That makes a pleasant change! But we've no time to chat – we've got to get the truck turned.'

'Away from the airfield?' Douglas queried at once. 'But Isobel and the others are flying home. Ortega's cleared it.'

Sam gave a short laugh. 'I'd have been disappointed if you hadn't made at least one objection!' he commented. 'But you do want to go back to Yorkshire with your wife, don't you? Then shut up and do as you're told–'

'Sam – and Joachim there – are going to drive you to the border,' Angela explained hurriedly, indicating one of the half-dozen uniformed men milling about watchfully. 'They've found a checkpoint that's poorly guarded, and a battle-scarred army truck under the command of a general will get through. Once over the border, you'll be met by someone from the British Consulate.'

'You're not coming with us?' Isobel exclaimed.

'I belong here.' Angela moved closer to Luis's side. 'I never intended to leave.'

'We'll contact your families,' Douglas promised, as the truck's engine throbbed noisily into life. 'Let them know you're both all right.'

Angela reached up to grasp their hands.

'Goodbye, and good luck!'

'Come one!' Sam bawled from the cab, revving the engine impatiently. 'If we don't get a move on we'll never get across that border!'

Chapter Twelve

Home For Christmas

'We're safe and well, Kirsty!' Isobel's voice rang out joyfully over the line. 'We're on our way home!'

No matter that it was the middle of the night, Kirsty went racing around the house rousing Janey, Alasdair and Robbie to talk to their mother and father on that precious telephone link.

During the next thirty or so hours, the telephone was rarely silent. More calls to and from South America, to Dorrie and Ailsa in Auchlanrick, to Douglas's elderly parents in Canada – and to Paul Ashworth, who had quietly taken charge of the practicalities.

'I know it's only half-past eight, and Paul's not collecting them from Leeds until ten,' Winifred muttered on the wintry November morning as she stood at the kitchen table sprinkling cherries into her cake mix. 'But if I don't keep busy, I'll do nowt but fidget!'

'I'm hopeless at waiting too,' Kirsty agreed

with feeling.

She and the children had been wide awake, dressed and breakfasted since before six o'clock. They had tried to pass the time by playing Snakes and Ladders – Robbie's choice – but when his heavy eyes had closed, the game had been quietly abandoned.

Janey had tiptoed upstairs to arrange the new quilt and a bowl of freshly-cut chrysanthemums in her parents' room, while Alasdair had braved the chill, foggy morning and disappeared for an early walk along the riverbank with the dog.

Kirsty eased a cushion under Robbie's head where he slept on the couch.

'He'll probably sleep for hours!' she whispered, joining Winifred at the table. 'I'll wash my hands and help you–'

The garden door crashed open and Alasdair burst inside with Teddy barking and tearing around his legs.

'They're here!' he yelled breathlessly, his cheeks scarlet with delight and cold. 'Mum and Dad are back!'

Janey galloped downstairs, Winifred dropped a scoop of brown sugar and Robbie woke up with a start, wondering what was going on.

His eyes widened as Paul shepherded Isobel and Douglas inside, their faces wreathed in smiles, and then the room erupted into a commotion of cries and hugs and laughter and questions. Everybody was talking at once, shouting to make themselves heard.

'Everything's just the same, Douglas,' Isobel murmured, gazing almost disbelievingly at him. 'We're home, and everything's just the same. Winifred's even baking for Christmas!'

'Ay, well, I've never been one for leaving things till the last minute,' the woman retorted gruffly, wiping her eyes with the corner of her apron. 'Sit yourselves down and I'll put the kettle on. I daresay you're parched for a decent cup of tea.'

Kirsty crept from the kitchen to leave the family alone, and Paul followed suit, joining her in the hall.

'They got the chance of an earlier flight.' He was beaming. 'Decided to surprise everyone.'

'It's wonderful!' She paused, half-turning. 'I'd better check Douglas's study. He's bound to–'

'Don't run away!' Paul pleaded. 'I have tried to be patient, but there'll never be a better day to ask–'

'Please, Paul,' she whispered, raising

imploring eyes. 'Don't.'

He bowed his head regretfully, disappoint-ment and futile longing a leaden weight in his chest.

'I only want your happiness,' he mur-mured. 'You know that, don't you?'

'Yes.' She swallowed the knot of sadness rising to her throat. 'I do.'

'What will you do now?' he inquired at length, making a monumental effort to concentrate on matters safe and mundane. 'Stay on here?'

'I'm not sure. I haven't a home now – or a job.'

She glanced at the closed kitchen door, from beyond which came the sounds of the family's laughter. She was suddenly sharply aware that she had a life, as well as a career, to rebuild.

'I've no idea what, or where, my future is going to be,' she admitted honestly. 'And it scares me.'

The whole family gathered at Chimneys for Christmas. Only Douglas's parents, who were too frail to make the long trip from Quebec, were absent.

'It's a shame, but when Isobel and Doug-las take the children over for a holiday next month, it'll make up for it,' Winifred remarked to Ailsa as they bustled around preparing for the Hogmanay celebrations.

The last day of the year had dawned crisp and clear, with bright wintry sunshine glittering on the frozen river. The two women had the house to themselves, except for Douglas and Harry Bell who were in the study continuing a chess game that had started on Christmas Eve.

Isobel and Dorrie had strolled to the station with the twins to meet Kirsty off the train, Paul and Graham were skating with the boys on the Beck, and Janey had dashed into town for a pair of spangly earrings.

'After they get back from Canada,' Winifred went on, carefully pressing Isobel's best embroidered tablecloth, 'will you be moving in?'

'I'm really considering it this time,' Ailsa confided, pausing in her task of slicing oranges and lemons for the punch bowl. 'I couldn't have left Auchlanrick before, but now that Dorrie's well, with a family of her own, and they've the chance of that lovely cottage at Kincarron...'

Her gaze strayed through the window to where Paul was gliding along, towing Robbie behind him.

''I only wish Kirsty was settled, too.' She sighed heavily. 'Paul was such a good influence on her. He's such a fine man. I really hoped they'd – but as soon as Isobel and Douglas got here, she was off. I gather she's practically living out of a suitcase in Birmingham,' she commented disapprovingly. 'And what happened at Christmas? She came for one day, then rushed off again.'

'That's because she didn't have much time to prepare for playing Cathy,' Winifred protested loyally.

Although Wuthering Heights would be mostly filmed in the television studios at Birmingham, the outdoor scenes were being done in and around Haworth, and Kirsty had been rushing back and forward.

'She's been working really hard this past month, you know,' Winifred reminded Ailsa.

'It's what she wants I suppose,' the other woman conceded, her eyes still wistful. 'But it's not a bit what I would have chosen for her.'

The three sisters had gossiped the entire way home from the station, stopping off for hot chocolate at the inn, and they were in high old spirits when they clattered into Chimneys later that afternoon.

'She's here!' Isobel announced to the family at large as she relieved Kirsty of her coat and scarf.

'But not for long!' Dorrie chipped in cheerfully, lifting Tom from his pram while Kirsty picked up Lucy for a cuddle. 'The film folk have been waiting to do a snowy-morning scene so she has to go back and work.'

'Surely not?' Ailsa exclaimed, disappointed. 'It's Hogmanay, after all.'

'That's rotten luck!' Alasdair chipped in.

'You'll miss the party, Auntie Kirsty!' added Janey.

'Enough, everybody!' She laughingly halted the protests with outstretched hands. 'The driver's not collecting me until after midnight. So we'll all be together to celebrate the New Year!'

After midnight, the festivities quietened and the family settled around the fire while Paul spun a spine-tingling tale about a headless horseman who haunted the nearby woods. Kirsty caught Isobel's eye, raised a finger to her lips and slipped away.

Hogmanay had made her reflective, and she wanted a little time alone.

Wandering from the house, she drifted

down the garden and out along the Beck. The frozen water and snowy banks were frosted and sparkling beneath the moon.

'Kirsty!'

The familiar voice stopped her where she stood.

Turning slowly, she saw Josh striding along the riverbank.

He halted a few yards from her and whole seconds of tense silence ticked away as they stared at each other, unsure what to do or say.

Josh cleared his dry throat.

'I went to Haworth. They told me a driver was coming to collect you. It wasn't difficult to take his place, not on New Year's Eve.'

Kirsty nodded wordlessly, startled by the rush of pure happiness singing through her at the very sight of him.

'How have you been?' he added.

'All right,' she got out shakily, her breathing almost non-existent. 'You?'

'Fine. No, not fine!' he amended vehemently, closing the distance which separated them and catching her shoulders with both hands. 'I've never been so miserable in my life!'

'It wasn't that I didn't trust you,' she mumbled unhappily. 'I – I just couldn't help being jealous.'

'I understand – now,' he confessed rue-fully, smiling at her for the first time. 'It's torn me apart imagining you up here with another man – even one who's just a friend. I didn't want him seeing you when I wasn't.'

'We've–' she began, but Josh's fingertips against her mouth silenced her.

'Right from the start, there's only been you, Kirsty. I've never wanted – never loved – anyone as I love you,' he breathed. 'I don't know what the future's going to be – or how we'll organise our lives. All I do know is that whatever lies ahead, I want us to share it.'

Kirsty smiled, gazing up at him.

'It's a new year,' she whispered, reaching to brush his lips with hers. 'A time for new beginnings.'

He gathered her in his arms and, pre-sently, they started back along the moonlit riverbank, casting but a single shadow upon the glistening snow...

The publishers hope that this book has given you enjoyable reading. Large Print Books are especially designed to be as easy to see and hold as possible. If you wish a complete list of our books please ask at your local library or write directly to:

Dales Large Print Books
Magna House, Long Preston,
Skipton, North Yorkshire.
BD23 4ND

This Large Print Book, for people
who cannot read normal print,
is published under the auspices of

THE ULVERSCROFT FOUNDATION